THE ANTITHESIS

HYMN OF THE MULTIVERSE 3

SHATTER STAR PRESS
ISBN 9781796985849

THREE
FALLEN

O
OF KIN

Yahweh Telei—;

EVERYTHING SEEMED SO ALIEN.

I was home—as *home* as I could be—and yet there was an aching in my chest that told me I shouldn't be here. Not here, not now. There were too many things happening all at once, and many of them were my doing.

My footsteps were soft against the bridge hall, but the ones behind me were heavy—powerful, formidable. And then they stopped.

I turned and saw my brother standing in the glass hall, looking out into the Ark. Light reflected from his cool, blue eyes as he marveled silently at all we'd done in his absence.

"The Commander is waiting for us," I said, urging him along.

Ixiah looked at me, expressionless. He appeared no older than the day he'd left, but there was an obvious difference. He wasn't an angel anymore, and it showed. The soft wisdom in his eyes had been replaced by a stoic gaze.

Lifelessness, *apathy*. The signature look of a scholar.

He said nothing, lowering his head and pressing on.

When my father had called the Court of Enigmus, I'd felt a fluttering in my chest at the chance of seeing Ixiah again. It'd been so long—five hundred years, but the excitement quickly turned to disappointment. We might as well been strangers.

But there was a flicker in his eyes, one of recognition—*feeling*—when he looked at me, albeit that was all I'd been afforded.

Lucifer was at his desk, staring out the window. The stack of papers next to him had grown exponentially since I'd been here last. He wasn't himself, but I couldn't blame him.

He turned at the sound of our entrance, settling a gaze of surprise on my brother. Lucifer had noticed the change, too.

"Thank you for coming," he said. "I wasn't expecting you so soon."

"I came the moment I was given word, Commander Raith."

Not Lucifer. *Commander Raith.* Once upon a time we were family.

Lucifer's eyes lowered to the clutter on his desk, burying his wounded arm deeper into his coat. The more he tried to hide it, the more obvious it became. Five days ago I'd cauterized it, and the stench of burning flesh always accompanied that memory. Lucifer had lost his hand because of me. Because I'd forgotten to give Qaira that sedative.

I never told him what I'd done; I was too ashamed.

"Can I get you anything to eat, or drink?" offered Lucifer.

Ixiah shook his head. "No, thank you."

I inched toward the door, but Lucifer caught me. "No, Yahweh. I'd like you to hear this as well."

I returned to my brother's side, exhaling slowly. We sat across the desk.

Lucifer's eyes darted between us, and he smiled mirthlessly. "You two almost look identical now."

Ixiah and I looked at each other, saying nothing. It was true. In a few hundred years I would be the age equivalent of when he'd joined the Court of Enigmus. They did not age past their assimilation. And then with trepidation I realized that one day I would look *older* than my brother.

"How much did your noble tell you?" asked Lucifer.

2

"Enough," said Ixiah.

"That scholar; she was Aipocinus' guardian, right?"

"Yes. Her name is Leid Koseling, and she was a scarlet guardian before our King expired. She's been under the supervision of my noble since." Although Ixiah said this with dispassion, there was a spark of something in his gaze. It was enough to let us know that he did not like Leid Koseling.

"Calenus is her appointed noble?" Lucifer asked, voice catching in his throat.

Ixiah nodded, seeming to anticipate his next question.

"He sent one of *his* to aid our enemies?"

Evidently Lucifer was hurt by that. The angels were allied with Calenus. He'd worked on Felor more times than I could count, and his recruitment of my brother was supposed to be a fortification of that alliance.

Ixiah held Lucifer's gaze, stony. "We are neutral, Commander Raith. Your race isn't the only one that we aid."

"*Your* race, you mean," Lucifer said, coolly.

Ixiah's façade broke then. He reclined in his seat, sighing. "Calenus sent Leid to a losing side. The odds were impossible. The Nehel weren't supposed to win. I'm surprised that I'm sitting here, really."

"Why would he send her to a losing side?"

"A passive form of punishment," said my brother, slightly amused. "She's caused some tumult in Exo'daius lately. Leid was cagey, and Calenus saw fit to have her sent away for a while. Despite her unruly behavior, she's a formidable war tactician and hasn't lost a single contract. A loss would have humbled her, or so my noble thought."

How cruel.

There was a lengthy moment of silence. I stood and headed for the coffee station near the door. I needed a cup.

"What will you do now?" asked Lucifer.

"That depends entirely on you. I was told that Leid and the Nehelian Regent are MIA."

Five days ago, my father shot Qaira in the stomach and he fell off the Ark. Leid jumped overboard with him. Although their plummet wasn't survivable, our search teams couldn't find them. We'd spent a day and a half skirting the tundra to no avail. Somehow they'd made it back to Sanctum.

"We haven't found them, no," Lucifer verified. "The only possibility is that they're in Sanctum."

"Then I will go there."

"Right now?"

"No. Right now I will return to the Court of Enigmus and discuss the matter with the others. I'll gather a team to recover Leid. You'll just have to wait a little while longer, Commander."

"That's fine."

Ixiah's eyes lowered to Lucifer's bandaged arm. "I'm very sorry that this happened to you. On behalf of the Court of Enigmus, I would like to formally apologize for the unprofessionalism that Leid Koseling has shown, and would also like to assure you that this isn't custom."

As I poured coffee, I wondered what would happen to Leid. I liked her, and Qaira, and the entire situation was almost too numbing to think about. I'd hidden most of how I felt from Lucifer and Ixiah—there was no arguing for Qaira's life anymore, not after what he'd done.

If only this story had begun differently, ended differently.

Lucifer nodded solemnly and Ixiah stood, cuing that their conversation was over.

"We'll be in touch, Lucifer."

Lucifer. He'd called him Lucifer, and then he'd smiled. Not a true smile, but the goodbye had been much warmer than the greeting.

"Do you need to be shown to the port?" my father asked, beginning to rise.

"No need. I'll find my way."

And then Ixiah was gone.

I stood at the coffee station, sipping from my cup.

My brother's appearance seemed to have invigorated Lucifer, as he'd finally begun to tend to that stack of paperwork. After a minute of silence, I too headed for the door, but just as I crossed the threshold, my father said, "Why didn't you tell me about her?"

I froze.

His tone hadn't been angry, but a soft question. I suspected he knew the answer already.

I turned, trying to think of a response that didn't sound treacherous. "I didn't want this to happen."

Lucifer only looked at me. It was hard to explain to him that after spending nearly half a year with Qaira and Leid, I had grown to know them, to *like* them. He wasn't questioning my allegiance—I'd already proven my loyalty by betraying Qaira five days ago. *But...*

"This must be very hard for you," he said.

I looked away, ashamed. He said nothing else and I retreated to the bridge.

My pager buzzed. I was needed at the medical ward. Namah had taken my place as Crylle physician, and I'd taken his as head doctor on the Ark. He wasn't pleased to hear that they weren't bringing him back in the foreseeable future. Lucifer didn't want me out of his sight. Crylle was not a safe place to be, especially now.

I moved down the bridge with my eyes on my feet, hoping that some suturing and amputations could away my thoughts. The war was essentially won, but the price of our victory had cost us much.

And I felt that burden more than anyone.

I
FRACTURED

Tulan steak, marinated poi and blackened saar.

Tae had made all three of my favorite things for dinner tonight, and all I did was push the plate aside. My sister hung her head and cried. But it wasn't her fault.

I couldn't eat. My stomach felt as heavy as iron, laced with a searing hot pain that no medication could touch. The doctors had told me I was lucky to be alive, but I didn't share their opinion.

I had failed; in more ways than one.

Leid had dragged me miles across the tundra, all the way back to Sanctum, and Ara's men had found us at the borderlands. I'd woken up two days ago at Eroqam Medical Facility—what was left of it, anyway—with a hole in my stomach, a subdural hematoma and a crushed leg. Leid had suffered no injuries.

They'd stopped the bleeding and stitched me up, performed surgery on my leg and gave me medication for the migraine that raged full-throttle all day every day, but there was nothing they could do for my spirit. It was gone, annihilated along with my city.

"Qaira."

I looked at Leid, who looked back at me with stern eyes.

"You need to eat something. You haven't eaten since you've been home."

My gaze drifted back to my plate. I wanted to eat—I really did. She didn't understand the pain. "I can't."

"You can. Put the food in your mouth and chew. You're going to die if you don't."

"Maybe that's what I want," I snapped, and her expression softened. "Have you ever thought about that?"

Tae cried even harder. My brother shook his head, muttered something under his breath, and left the table.

The softness in Leid's expression faded. "Self-pity doesn't suit you."

Neither did the cast, or these bandages, or *failure*.

"Will you at least drink some water?"

I reached for my crutches. Without another word I hobbled out of the dining room. I needed silence; Leid was making my migraine even worse.

In ten seconds flat, she caught up to me, carrying my abandoned dinner plate. "You're going to eat, even if I have to force this down your throat."

"Leave me alone."

"I won't. Not until you get some food in you. The doctor said you have to keep eating or else your stomach acid will disrupt the healing process."

I sighed, giving up.

In my room, Leid helped me into bed and I leaned against the headboard. She set the plate on my lap and took a seat in the armchair, watching. I grabbed the fork with a grimace and stabbed a piece of steak, lifting it to my lips. It tasted so good that I almost melted, but as soon as I swallowed the burning in my gut intensified. I laid there, unable to do anything except ride the worst pain I'd ever felt. It was so paralyzing that I couldn't even scream.

Leid noticed the look on my face and winced. "Just a few more bites, *please*."

Instead, I threw the plate at the wall. Dinner and porcelain scattered across the floor.

Leid hung her head.

"How did this happen?" I stammered. "How could this have happened?"

It wasn't supposed to be like this. I wasn't supposed to be laying near-dead in this bed, with half of Sanctum in ruins beyond my window. We should have been celebrating the angels' defeat. I should have been giving my victory speech.

My vision blurred as tears glazed my eyes, but I choked them back. I was pathetic enough already.

"I didn't drag you back here so you could give up," Leid said. "Your people need you. They need to know what to do next."

"I don't know what to do next!" I shouted. "Why don't *you* tell me what to do, *Advisor* Koseling?"

Leid looked away, wiping her eyes. "Surrender."

I blanched. "What?"

"There's nothing else we can do. You have to surrender."

Those words had a stronger paralyzing effect than the pain. For a second I couldn't even feel my stomach. "Never."

"Your army is gone, half your city is in ruins, and over a hundred thousand of your people are dead. Do you want to lose everything? Kill everyone?"

I'd already lost everything, and the truth hurt worse than any wound. "You could do it."

"… Do what?"

"Destroy the Ark. You told Raith that you could do it."

She looked at me as if I'd just slapped her. "I can't."

"Can't, or won't?"

"Both. I only did that to save you. I'm not going to kill an entire race for winning fair and square."

"If you don't, they'll kill me."

"They won't kill you if you surrender."

"I'm not surrendering."

Leid clenched her jaw, saying nothing.

"And I didn't ask you to save me," I said through my teeth. "I would rather die than face defeat. That has always been the Nehel way. In hindsight I have no idea why I ever put my faith in you. We lost, even with you here."

Anger had taken control of my mind. I'd regretted saying that the moment it left my mouth, but the damage was already done. Leid stared at me like I'd ripped out her heart and stomped it into red mush. Blood tears trickled down her cheeks, and she left my room with her face in her hands.

"No, wait—" I reached for her, but she was already gone. *"Leid, wait! I'm sorry!"*

Silence.

I cursed under my breath as the searing in my gut resumed. It placated me, and soon I fell into restless sleep, dreaming of Maghir's Ocean.

***

Our craft swept over the wreckage of Upper Sanctum, a sea of rubble and high-rise carcasses. Streets were buried by debris and covered in smoke from still-burning fires deep below the ruins. The sky was the color of ashen coal, still and somber. Everything seemed dead.

Everything *was* dead.

Ara and I watched the scenery pass with solemnity. We hadn't spoken at all since our departure from Eroqam, and the tension was getting thicker by the second.

We were on our way to the pyres, where a hundred thousand bodies lay waiting to be burned. Usually pyres were individual ceremonies, but the body count was too high. We would burn our dead in bulk.

In bulk. What an ugly phrase.

This would be my first appearance since the battle, and the thought of facing my people made me tremble. I would have to give a speech, *on crutches*, assuring them that everything would be alright. I'd have to preach hope and other worthless crap that I didn't believe. And they would look on at me in anger and disappointment, wishing I had died in battle.

The migraine moved to my forehead, its pressure like stout fingers pushing out my eyes. I wanted to slam my head through the windshield so everything would end.

As we descended through the pyre fields, my brother glanced around the cabin. "Where's Leid?"

"I don't know."

He stared, waiting for an explanation.

"We had a fight. She took off this morning and I haven't seen her since."

"What did you fight about?" he asked, looking out the window.

I hesitated. "She wants me to surrender."

"You should."

Ara, too?

"Sanctum can't take another hit like this. We're done, Qaira. We gave it our best fight, but we're done."

The pyres were being prepped by our incinerators, and clouds of smoke billowed into the sky like black torpors. It covered our craft, and neither of us could see. When we landed, Ara exited first and offered his hand as I steadied my crutches.

"It should have been you," I said quietly.

"What?"

"You should have been Regent."

He stared at me, abashed. I limped away, disappearing through the smoke.

***

Corpses covered in white sheets, laid across planks, were carried up the ramp to the pyres by groups of *Yetans*—priests of Maghir— while the audience sang Moritorian hymns. Their voices rose with the smoke, entrenching a cadence of sorrow. The stench of burning flesh made my stomach churn as I stood stone-faced with a row of officials behind the ramp.

The smoke cleared and I saw Lakash's wife and daughter in the front row, their faces tired and tear-stained. Neither of them looked at me.

And then I looked at other people's faces. Their pain screamed at me, and I thought about everything I'd done—every order I'd given, every decision I had made without any consideration as to whom it would affect. For a decade I had led them, but I had never *seen* them.

I'd struggled with a speech for the pyre all morning, but now I knew exactly what to say.

The hymns died, giving way to the dozen speeches that followed. I was last, so I had to sit through another forty minutes of transparent promises of rebuilding and becoming stronger than before. Hope and transcendence and blah blah blah. At one point I scoffed and some of the officials turned to look at me.

Their promises meant nothing, and it angered me how they spewed lies to our people. I was the one that had to fulfill these promises, and I couldn't. There were no repercussions of their false comfort. They would look like heroes and I would be the asshole that couldn't meet their goals.

They even spoke for me. *The Regent this; the Regent that*— the Regent was a fucking idiot who'd just destroyed his own city. I'd promised to crush the angels and all I'd ended up crushing was our world. And my leg.

And then it was my turn.

I hobbled to the ramp as the audience watched me silently, keeping my gaze down in fear of seeing the pity in their eyes. No one needed to tell me I looked like shit.

The grass was easy to get across, but the gravel posed a challenge. One of my crutches got stuck between loose rocks and I almost fell, but a guard rushed to steady me. I shoved him away, snarling. "I'm fine."

He backed away at my rejection.

It took me almost ten minutes to get up the ramp because I refused any help. Once there, I looked over the eighty thousand

Nehelians who had gathered at the pyre fields, a sea of faces almost stretching to the Aeroway.

I inhaled, and began.

"I have failed you, Sanctum, in more ways than you know. I am not the man you think I am. I've *never* been that man, and I have ruled without empathy or regard for causality."

Confusion emanated from the crowd. People looked at each other, questioningly.

Ara stood, narrowing his eyes. I had to hurry.

"If my father could see me now, he would cry. He would cry because the son he'd always believed in has destroyed the only thing he'd left behind. He trusted me with Sanctum, but he may as well have given Sanctum to a child."

My brother said something to his soldiers, pointing at me. They headed for the ramp, and the crowd began to murmur.

"I could have killed Commander Raith! I had him at my feet, but I chose a minute more of his suffering over the lives of my men! Sanctum, we are doomed! *We are doomed because I am your leader!*"

"He's lost it! Get him off the stage—!"

A guard approached me, gingerly, and asked if I could hand him the microphone and step off the ramp. I told him to fuck off.

Cameras flashed as another group of guards tackled me, ripping the mic from my hand. It took five of them to apprehend me and drag me from the stage, all the while I screamed and thrashed, drowned out by the thunder of hysteria. Over and over I shouted the same thing with eyes raised to the bruised sky, like a prayer for a deaf, frigid god:

"SANCTUM, PLEASE FORGIVE ME!"

II
PREDATION

FOR THE REST OF THE DAY, I'D LOCKED myself in my room. The phone rang off the hook and I heard my sister telling Sanctum PB to leave us alone, her pleas shriller and shriller each time.

Ara was forced to spend the afternoon at Eroqam dealing with the fallout from my episode of *post-traumatic stress*, or so he'd deemed it.

I was waiting for the officials to motion for my impeachment, but that motion never came. Instead I was glorified for my freak-out. *Idolized.* The crowd had been moved by my confession, and the media quickly swooped in to fuel the flames. According to them, my melt-down was the product of my guilt; I was heartbroken that I couldn't protect my city and its people. Moreover, the Yetans preached that Maghir had brought me back from the dead, as I'd returned from the Ark alive, despite impossible odds and fatal injuries.

I'd gone to the pyres looking for reparation, to be made a pariah. Instead I was deified even more. What the fuck was wrong with everyone?

My sister had forced me to drink some kind of herbal tea that had smelled like moss and tasted like swamp water, and it was burning the shit out of my stomach. I lay in bed and watched the light change across my bedroom wall, panting and wishing for death.

I fell asleep before dinner, and awoke at sunset to someone's hand sliding across my chest. Leid sat at my bedside, looking me over with concern. The dying sun bled through my window and cast an orange haze over us, making the moment surreal. The violet of her eyes was muted by the light, and now they glittered like gold.

"I thought you were gone," I said, nearly whispering.

"I almost was," she said, lowering her gaze. "But I couldn't leave you. I heard about what happened. I saw your speech on the news. Qaira, I'm sorry. I should have been there."

"Don't apologize. It was my fault."

Silence; Leid curled into bed with me, laying her head against my chest.

"I saw Lakash's family today," I said. "Their faces still haunt me."

She said nothing.

"Is this what it feels like?" I asked. "The guilt; I can't take it. It feels like my heart is being wrapped in barbed wire."

"It hurts," she whispered. "It's supposed to. It's the only way that we can learn. *Change.*"

"Marry me."

She looked up, stunned. "What?"

"I want to marry you. Stay here with me, in Sanctum."

Leid searched my eyes for any disingenuity, but found none. I was serious. She'd dragged me through fire and over spikes to make me a better man. In many ways, I owed her my life. Without her I'd still be a junkie derelict, unfit for anything.

And then she started to cry. Not exactly the response I was hoping for.

"You don't want to?" I asked, crestfallen.

"No," she said, shaking her head, hiding her face. "It's not that. I... I want to. Qaira, I want to be with you more than anything but...but I *can't.*"

I reached for her, and then my radio buzzed. I glanced at it, but dismissed the call. This was more important.

It kept ringing.

"Get it," Leid said, wiping her face.

I reached for my crutches, but then she motioned for me to stop and retrieved it herself. When she tossed it to me, I pressed the receiver button. "Go ahead."

"Qaira, where are you?"

It was my brother. He sounded panicked.

"At home."

"We have visitors. They're at the northern spire."

"I don't want to talk to anyone. Send them away."

"They're not taking no for an answer. They claim they're from something called the Court of Enigmus, and they're asking for you. You need to get down here. They don't look right. One of them… looks like an angel."

I looked at Leid, and she only hung her head. Suddenly her sadness made sense. She knew this was going to happen. Lucifer had called her lot and now they were here to take her away.

But I'd promised that I wouldn't let her go that easily, and I always kept my promises.

"I'll be down in a minute."

I severed the call and grabbed my crutches, struggling to my feet. "Stay here," I told her. "Hide if you have to."

"Qaira, whatever you're planning, you can't—"

"I'm not letting them take you away. They'll have to kill me before that happens."

"They *will* kill you."

"Let me talk to them first. They asked for me, not you."

She sank to my bed. "Be careful."

I nodded, heading out.

***

All eyes were on me the moment I'd appeared in the foyer. That was because everyone had spent two full minutes listening to the sound of my crutches from the elevator.

Ara stood at the foot of the stairs, staring at our guests. Three of our guards were backed against the wall, their guns scattered at

17

the scholars' feet. Disarmed, but not slain. They weren't here to kill.

There were two of them, clad in black coats, a glowing red sigil adorning their breasts. It was like they had set fire to their clothes, but the flames had been contained to only one place. I didn't believe in magic, but this was really challenging that belief.

Neither of them said a thing, staring placidly.

"Hi," I said.

The angel scholar stepped forward. At first glance I could have sworn it was Yahweh, but he looked a little older. A little *meaner*. His cold, blue gaze started at my crutches and slowly made its way to my face. "Regent Qaira Eltruan?"

"Yes."

"My name is Ixiah Telei, scholar of the Court of Enigmus." He nodded to his partner. "This is Ziranel Throm, also a scholar."

Ziranel was not angel-borne—pale skinned with hair as black as Leid's, cut unevenly to his jaw, and eyes the color of fire. From what I could tell, their society of scholars was a mosaic of alien races. *Aliens-turned-Vel'Haru.*

"You're Yahweh's brother."

"I am," said Ixiah, stone faced. "If you know that, then you must know why we're here."

"I have an idea, yes."

"Should we continue with formalities, or would you care to hand Leid over and spare us all the time?"

"Leid is not my property, so I can't just hand her over. She's already told me that she doesn't want to go with you."

Ixiah smiled, and it was scary. The smile was warm, inviting, but it was accompanied by the look of a sociopath. Clearly he was nothing like Yahweh, and there was little chance of talking him out of what he'd come here to do.

"Do you know who we are, Regent?" That question was a threat.

My lip curled. "Do you know who *I* am?"

Ziranel stepped forward, leaning into his partner. "Stop fooling around. We'll find her ourselves."

"I haven't given you permission to enter my home," I said.

Ziranel grinned, his sharp canines gleaming under fluorescence. "We don't need permission. A perk of being at the top of the food-chain. You're guilty of contract violation, but we'll let you live if you step aside."

Ara looked at me, his expression relaying that I should step aside. Instead, I pulled out my gun. The scholars seemed amused.

Ixiah scoffed. "Really?"

"You can't tell me that a bullet between your eyes wouldn't sting," I chided.

"Qaira, *please*," begged Ara.

"Aim your gun at them, Commandant. That's an order."

With a wince, my brother did as I'd commanded.

Ziranel and Ixiah looked between us, laughing softly. Namah had been right, but Leid was nothing like these assholes. Now I knew why she was so frightened, and I would never forgive myself if I let these savages take her away.

"Leid is staying here," I said, the look in my eyes daring them to take another step. "Kindly take your leave."

"Let me explain what's going to happen," Ixiah began, climbing the first step. "You are going to *think* about pulling that trigger, but before your brain can even send a message to your finger, I'll have already snapped your neck."

"Talk is cheap, white. Show me what you've got."

I pulled the trigger, but he was gone. A fraction of a second later I was against the wall, his fingers curled around my neck. We were nose-to-nose.

"Believe me now?" he whispered.

I narrowed my eyes. Ixiah's head didn't explode, but he'd felt *something*. Whatever it was, it surprised him, and he released me with a gasp.

And then a blur hit him and he was thrown across the foyer, landing headfirst into a pillar. His collision left a giant crack in the stone.

My brother dropped his gun and backed away, unable to believe his eyes. That blow should have killed anyone. Anyone but a scholar, and now Ara knew.

The blur had been Leid.

She shielded me, snarling. "Stay back."

Ixiah got to his feet, wiping away the blood that trickled from a nasty gash across his forehead. He sneered. "Your plaything has a smart mouth."

His partner took a step forward, but Leid held out a hand. "Zira, *don't*."

Ziranel froze.

They were afraid of her. Why were two guardians afraid of one?

"Leid, you can't stay here," reasoned Ixiah. "Calenus has ordered that you return. If you don't come with us, we'll return with *him*."

Her hand fell limp at her side. She looked at the ground.

No.

"Promise not to hurt Qaira or his brother."

"We didn't want to hurt them," said Ziranel. "They wouldn't step aside."

He reached out to her, and, reluctantly, she descended the stairs.

"Wait," I breathed, grabbing her arm. She pulled away. "Leid, don't go."

She looked over her shoulder, smiling through tears. "I'll never forget you."

I watched, paralyzed, as Ixiah and Ziranel guided her toward the exit. I would never see her again, and there was nothing I could do to stop them. I'd never felt so powerless in my entire life. What would happen to her? What kind of punishment did scholars serve for violating a contract? Were they marching Leid to her death?

As they opened the door, I shouted, "I'll surrender to the angels!"

All three of them froze, looking back at me. Leid was shocked, the others confused.

"I'll let the Ark into The Atrium. They can have it. They can have everything," I said. When neither of them responded, I rasped, "What else do you want? What else can I give you?"

"Leid is not for sale," Ixiah said, but the fire in his eyes was gone. "And orders are orders. As far as I can tell, bargaining with your surrender is pointless, considering you've already lost."

"If you take her, I will make their colonization insufferable. We will attack the angels at every opportunity, whittling them away. How many are left after our battle? How many have died already? I can promise that your brother's life will be a miserable one. They may have won access to my world, but the war is far from over."

Something changed on Ixiah's face. He and Ziranel shared a look. Their hesitation had sparked a cinder of hope.

"If you let her stay, I will *invite* the angels into our world. Their colonization will be peaceful. *Safe.* Sanctum will not attack them."

Ziranel glared at Ixiah, realizing that he was considering my offer. "We don't have the power to decide that. A scholar has never left our court."

"Leid is trouble, Zira. She's an exception."

"Calenus will not like this."

"I will deal with him."

He stepped back, shocked. "So, you're doing it?"

Ixiah said nothing, gazing at me. There was no cruelty on his face. He looked like Yahweh more than ever. "You will give the angels peace, Regent?"

"I am a man of my word, scholar."

He released Leid's arm, nudging her forward. "Consider the contract voided and Scholar Leid Koseling excommunicated from Exo'daius. I will return to the Ark with the news. I suggest you schedule a meeting with Commander Raith in the near future to negotiate terms of a settlement."

Ziranel released Leid as well, but with reluctance. Leid had said that scholars were neutral; loyal to no world except their own. Twice now I'd seen evidence against that claim. Ixiah was not an angel anymore, but he was willing to save them. And, judging by Ziranel's disquieted demeanor, that decision would come with a heavy price.

But it was neither my business nor my problem. Leid was here to stay; that was all I cared about.

The scholars vacated the foyer, leaving Leid at the door. She looked up at me, stunned, unable to believe that I had just negotiated for her freedom. My brother and his men regrouped, heading for the elevator. Ara looked back and nodded before he slipped away, his expression alluding to an entire bottle of Cardinal in his near-future.

And then Leid and I were alone, me at the top of the steps, her at the bottom. We stared at each other, silent, overwhelmed by thoughts of *what next*. Nine months ago she had come to my world with the task of making sure it stayed in my possession, and I had just given it away, all for her. There'd been no pain or shame in that decision, either.

Because Leid Koseling was worth more than anything I had. Anything I could give.

I had absolutely no idea what the future held for me, or for Sanctum, but none of that mattered now because *she* would be in it.

O

FAREWELL

Yahweh Telei—;

LUCIFER WAS COUGHING SO HARD THAT he almost retched. Ixiah had announced that Qaira was letting the angels into The Atrium while he was sipping tea.

I couldn't blame him for his shock—I hardly believed it myself.

"He agreed to an Archaean settlement so long as we let him keep Leid."

"Keep Leid?" Lucifer repeated, still coughing.

Ixiah nodded. "It's a double-win. You get your world and the Court of Enigmus gets some peace and quiet."

"Calenus agreed to that?"

Ixiah hesitated. "He will."

Lucifer looked questioningly at him, but said nothing else. He knew better than to pry at Vel'Haru affairs. We all did.

"What exactly *is* Qaira Eltruan?" asked Ixiah.

Lucifer tilted his head. "What do you mean?"

"He did something to me; with his mind. He made my thoughts fuzzy."

My father looked at me.

"Qaira has the ability of what I like to call *brain apoptosis*," I explained. "He releases high energy radiation, triggered by thought, which… well, can make people's heads explode."

"My head didn't explode. I just got confused."

"You're Vel'Haru. It must affect you differently. Usually it's fatal."

Ixiah reclined in his seat, rubbing his chin. "Interesting."

"I suppose that's one word for it," muttered Lucifer. "I don't know if I can trust a settlement. This all seems completely unlike him."

"He sounded sincere," said Ixiah, "but if there's any trouble, let me know."

"What happens next?"

"He should contact you shortly. What you do from there is not my concern, but I imagine you two will meet and negotiate."

Lucifer nodded. "Thank you, Ixiah. You don't know how much this means to me. To us."

"I do, and that's why I did it." He stood. "The Court is expecting me. Zira's already briefing them. Yahweh, could you walk me out?"

Me? "Uh, yes, sure."

Lucifer bid us both goodbye as we stepped onto the bridge, and then we were alone. We walked side-by-side toward the port, silent, awkward, wanting to speak but not knowing what to say.

"How's mother?" he asked, finally.

"Not so good."

"Worse?"

I nodded. "I haven't seen her for two years, but word is that she's on a regimen of antipsychotics."

Ixiah looked away, sadly. "Two years?"

"It's hard," I whispered. "It's hard to see her."

Because seeing her meant that I had to see *him*. And I saw him once a day already.

It was never a huge scene, only an indifferent nod to each other, but every time I saw him I thought about what had happened; what had happened before Lucifer had taken me under his wing. And I was sure that Ixiah's memories of our father were even worse.

In a sense it was his fault that Ixiah had left. Yes, there had been a negotiation, but Calenus would have never placed my brother on the table if he hadn't wanted to leave already. Like Lucifer to me, Calenus had saved him from years of abuse and neglect.

And now he was something else, something special. Ixiah looked the same, but spoke and carried himself with the sharp intellect of a scholar.

A scholar. It was still so hard to believe that he was one of them. It seemed like yesterday that he was flunking school and getting into fights, disappearing for days and having guards drag him home, shivering and emaciated. But so much had happened since he left, and he felt that, too.

"I never told you this," he began, hesitating. "I'm sorry that I left you. *With them*. I wasn't given much of a choice, but…"

"It's fine," I assured him, trying to smile. "It all worked out in the end for both of us."

"It did," he said, smiling as well, gazing out through the glass hall as we traversed it. "This is all so incredible."

I said nothing, letting him marvel. We left the hall and arrived at the port. Soldiers and civilians passed us by, nodding, but none of them recognized Ixiah. Not anymore. They had no idea that he'd just saved us all. And they never would.

Lucifer had arranged a craft that would take him to Crylle. He would find a portal there and return to Exo'daius. I didn't know when I'd see him again. Maybe never.

"Namah will be very upset that he didn't get to see you," I noted as he headed up the ramp.

Ixiah laughed. "Where is he?"

"At Crylle's hospital. You should stop in and visit him or he'll mope around for weeks."

"I might."

Once upon a time Namah and Ixiah had been school mates. Best friends. More than that, even. Yet another thing my father hated about his oldest son—his indiscrimination of love.

We didn't say farewell as he boarded the craft, only looked at each other as the doors slid shut. It was bad luck to say goodbye, at least for us. A goodbye affirmed the chance that we might never meet again.

The craft left the dock, floating slowly from the hangar. I watched until it descended out of sight, fading in the darkness. I smiled through sadness.

Qaira and Lucifer were going to negotiate. The war had ended without any more blood. Things had taken a turn for the better overnight.

As I left the hangar and ventured through *Nostra*—the eastern civilian sector, I wondered if Qaira would ever forgive me. I wondered if we would find a place on The Atrium that felt like home. I still remembered Felor, even now.

And then I wondered if this was really the *happily ever after* that everyone was hoping for.

III
LAID TO REST

THE MINUTES TICKED BY AS RAITH AND I SAT IN Eroqam's conference room. Neither of us had said a thing so far. We were supposed to be discussing the angel settlement, but all we did was stare daggers at each other.

My crutches rested on the table beside me. One of them shifted, about to fall, and I steadied it. Lucifer scratched at the bandage on his handless arm. We'd done this to each other—all this damage, only to end up here. It was funny and infuriating all at once.

Lucifer's eyes slid to the clock on the wall, and he sighed. "Are you going to say anything?"

"You first."

"You're the one who invited me down here."

"I said I wanted to hear your terms. So let's hear them."

The daggers in Lucifer's eyes turned to bullets. I could tell he wanted to swing at me, and a small part of me hoped that he would.

Instead we looked away.

"This isn't working," he muttered.

"Nope."

Time for Plan B.

***

"The Regent is giving you the upper layers of The Atrium," said Leid, reading from the document that I'd written up the night before. "The second highest layer has an abundance of resources for agricultural endeavors, so food won't be an issue for your people anymore."

"Your mines are located on the lower levels," said Lucifer, but he spoke to Leid and not me. "We need materials to build our cities."

Leid shot me a glance.

"You can have a quarter of our mines," I said. "But giving you that much will cost us, considering we have completely rebuild Sanctum after your attack."

"You mean *your* attack."

Daggers.

Yahweh cleared his throat, drawing our attention. Leid and the kid had stepped in as mediators, since we refused to speak to each other. "Regent, the metal alloys you used when we upgraded your crafts; they were extracted from the lower regions, too, right?"

"Right."

"To my understanding, most of the lower layers haven't been mined."

"It's too cold."

There were seven layers of The Atrium. Sanctum rested on the fourth. After the sixth, all of our machinery froze. We'd speculated for years that there were tons of deposits waiting to be mined, but no one could think of a way to overcome the subzero climate.

Leid looked at Yahweh, thoughtful. "Are you suggesting that the Archaeans mine the metals from the lowest regions?"

Yahweh nodded. "We don't want to intrude on your resources. But I think that if we work together, we might be able to obtain minerals from the lower regions—possibly more than enough to sustain both of our cities."

"Do you have drilling machinery that can operate at absolute zero?" It probably wasn't absolute zero, but it sure felt like it.

Lucifer and Yahweh shared a look, smiling.

"Yes, we do," said the kid.

I hesitated with a response, recalling that the angels had destroyed their last world with technology. The same technology that they were proposing to me.

… But we *could* use that metal.

"Qaira, what do you think?" pressed Leid.

"Alright, fine."

"We'll stay on the Ark until we have access to those mines," said Lucifer. "I won't impede on Sanctum's reconstruction."

"How thoughtful of you."

Leid kicked my broken leg, and I winced.

"Next topic?" Yahweh inquired, moving us along.

"We're back to food," Leid announced after a glance at the sheet. "Since we're giving you the upper layers, we will require a third of the agriculture and a fourth of the fish. The rest of our resources come from the lower layers, so that's all."

Lucifer arched a brow. "Fish?"

"Ysimel," Leid repeated, this time in Archaean. Our negotiations were being carried out in Nehelian.

"How much does your population consume per year?"

"A thousand grulas," I said. "But I'm willing to halve that so they don't go extinct."

"You have quite a few leriza farms in the upper layers," noted Yahweh, looking at the list. "If we share those as well, your city won't have to deprive itself of… *fish.*"

I reclined in my seat with an encumbered sigh. "I don't think we can accurately outline an agreement until you settle in and see how things go. It's not the sharing that I'm concerned about, it's your numbers."

Lucifer nodded. "If you're scared of overpopulation, what would you say to birth regulation?"

I stared, saying nothing. Telling my people that they weren't allowed to have kids wasn't going to win me any points.

"We've been doing it for centuries," he explained, sensing my unease. "We had to on our interstellar voyage, as the Ark could only sustain so many. We used intravenous birth control. "

"Your people actually agreed to that?"

"Why wouldn't they? They took into account that creating a child and having it suffer was more heinous a crime than not having a child."

"Sanctum holds a lot of pride in its children. It's custom for families to have them. Telling Nehelians that they can't have children is like telling them to clip their wings."

"You don't have to deny them any children," argued Lucifer. "But set a maximum amount of children per family. That way your population won't expand further than what your world can support."

"The only reason why my world couldn't support them is because of you."

He smiled at my contempt. "The fact still remains, Regent. I'm only offering suggestions that might ease your concern. The angels will continue regulating their births, and you can do whatever you want."

"There is one more thing," Yahweh said, breaking the silence that had followed. "We need to borrow your scholar. Well, I suppose she's not your *scholar* anymore, but we still need to borrow her."

I lifted a brow. "What for?"

"Planetary comparison," Yahweh said. At the sight of the cluelessness on my face, he added, "Normally we would hire a scholar to help us compare your planet's chemical properties with Felor's. Considering your circumstance, I would rather have Leid do that for us than bring another scholar here. I imagine things would get, well, *complicated*."

"I don't know if I have access to Euxodia anymore," said Leid, morose.

Yook-sod-ee-a?

"How can you tell?" Yahweh asked.

She closed her eyes and I could have sworn I'd felt a humming in my chest, like she was doing something to the air. The others felt it, too, judging by the surprise on their faces.

"I do. I suppose they can't keep me out. I'm still Vel'Haru."

"What's Euxodia?" I asked, since apparently I was the only one who didn't know.

"Our library," Leid said, smiling, and I remembered the talk we'd had in her first few weeks of being here. "The physical library is in Exo'daius, but our knowledge is linked together via our resonance. We make the information available through a conscious stream. Almost like a shared dreamscape."

I blinked. "Oh."

"And Ixiah has made the information which you seek available."

"So you will help us?" asked Yahweh.

She nodded. "And thank you for considering my circumstance."

Our negotiations were concluded when Lucifer declared that the Ark would enter The Atrium's airspace this evening, and I promised that our patrol would stand aside.

This was it. It was actually happening.

Lucifer and Yahweh left Eroqam with their guards, and Leid and I sat alone in the conference room. She was smiling at me.

"What?" I asked.

"You did very well, Qaira."

"Yeah, who knew I'd be so great at surrendering?"

"Don't look it at like that. You're negotiating for peace, and that's quite a feat."

"Feat?"

"Peace in The Atrium. You've brought the world peace after almost a century of war, and your people will never forget you for it."

She always made everything sound so pretty. Even my defeat.

I glanced at my watch. "What now?"

"Now we have a meeting with the Department of Sanitization. They're asking what you want to do about the wreckage at the Agora."

That meeting was going to take a while. I rose from the chair with a grimace, grabbing for a crutch. I was getting a little better at maneuvering with my cast. It came off in two weeks, but until then I was crippled.

Leid waited by the door, and together we headed for the Commons. All of our meetings were being held at Eroqam until we could rebuild Parliament. It was completely leveled from battle— along with everything else in Upper Sanctum. Everything except for Eroqam.

"What are we doing about lunch? It's half-past noon."

"Your secretary is catering *Tervat*," Leid said quickly, having anticipated that question.

Ugh, Tervat *again*. But I couldn't be picky, since that was the only decent restaurant still standing. Their business was probably booming.

Thinking about that left me solemn. I still mourned the Sanctum that had been—all the places I would never see again. I'd promised to rebuild our city bigger and better than ever, and maybe that would happen, but so much of my life was now just a memory. The only cushioning was that Leid was here, and here to stay.

As if reading my thoughts, she reached for my hand, fingers lacing mine.

We smiled.

IV

A ROAD LESS PERILOUS

"THE COMPOUND THAT WE'VE SYNTHETICALLY PRODUCED has the same effect as malay, but without fatal consequences. You see, the addictive component of the drug stimulates the neural symposium pathway in the brain, releasing YTF-alpha into the synaptic cleft, which gives off euphoria."

As Yahweh pointed at the projection screen with as much enthusiasm as a kid at a candy store, I rolled my pen along the desk, resisting the urge to shove it through my head. Three hours of a pharmacology lesson could do that to you.

None of this made a bit of sense. All I saw on that projection screen was an anatomical diagram of a head that someone had sliced in half, with a bunch of blue and red squiggly lines across it. But I was just retarded, because Raith was nodding every other minute, like he totally understood everything the kid was saying.

The bottom line was that Yahweh had designed a synthetic drug that mimicked malay, but didn't have fatal withdrawal symptoms. That had been good enough for me, but he'd insisted on explaining everything.

"Malay also acts as a kinase effector that works on the muscles of the lungs by phosphorylating the contraction pathway. After long-term use, the body stops providing its own intermediates and relies on the malay instead."

I leaned into my hand, sighing loudly.

"The synthetic drug we've designed differs by its substituents on the aromatic ring—"

And now we were looking at a bunch of sticks and circles. And letters.

"—where our not-so-polar carbonyl replaces the reducing agent of the malay. Therefore our drug does not act as a lung-contraction catalyst."

Yay.

At last, he was done. "What do you think?"

They looked at me, and I sat up straight. "The only word I understood from that entire spiel of yours was *brain*, so I'm probably not the right person to ask."

Lucifer laughed. "Where's your smarter half this afternoon, Regent?"

"Stuck at Enoria. It's finals week." Usually she dealt with shit like this, but alas, here I was. "Give me a copy of everything you just said and I'll run it by her. I'm sure she'll have some questions."

Yahweh was looking at me like I'd just ripped his favorite toy from his hand and stomped it to pieces in front of him. "You didn't understand *anything* I said?"

"You made a drug that acts like malay but doesn't kill people. Got it."

The kid sighed. "I don't even know why I bother."

"That drug could open doors to new treatment programs," said Lucifer. "The Plexus is building a new wing, and with your approval, we could transform it into a rehabilitation center."

"Don't we need to do some testing on it first? Make sure it's safe?"

"Of course. The entire purpose of us being here was to persuade you into signing off on a clinical trials program."

I hesitated as Yahweh handed me a type-set of his presentation. I didn't want to agree to anything until Leid saw this. "Give me a day to think on it. I'll call the Plexus tomorrow afternoon."

"Call my office," said Yahweh. "I'll be there all day handling paperwork."

To think that our medical science headquarters was run by a kid. Not just any kid, but still.

Yahweh Telei—*Dr.* Telei—was the CEO of the *Plexus*, a venture of medical and pharmaceutical research that both of our cities funded. It was the only place in the world where Nehelians *and* angels worked alongside each other. We were segregated otherwise, even after ten years since the angels had moved in. But the Plexus offered a glimmer of hope that that might change someday.

As they gathered their things and began for the door, Lucifer murmuring for me to take a look at this year's leriza farming projection when I had the time, I rushed down the hall to my next meeting. My secretary flagged me down.

"You've got a call, Regent."

"Take a message. I'm already late."

"It's your wife."

Sigh.

I detoured to my office. "Connect her through."

"Yes, sir."

I closed the door and touched the blinking rune on the crystal sphere atop my desk. We had upgraded our communications system several years ago. Like the Archaeans, we used a telepathically-wired technology called *Aeon*.

What?

Well hello to you, too. I hope this isn't how you answer all of your calls?

No, just you. You're special.

I'm going to be late tonight.

You've been late every night this week.

Blame my tenure.

When do you think you'll be home?

I don't know. Seven; maybe eight?

What about dinner?

It's in the freezer. Put the pan in the oven if you get hungry before I'm home.

No, it's fine. I'll wait for you.

You're afraid of the oven.

Am not.

Well put the pan in at six-thirty. I don't want to wait when I get home.

Anything else?

Nope, that's it. I'll see you tonight.

Apparently my job was never-ending. Leid had left Parliament and signed on as a Biomolecular professor at Enoria Academy five years ago, and I'd been putting frozen dinners in the oven ever since.

She'd let Epa go, stating that we didn't need a maid with just the two of us. She found servants distasteful—a flaunt of wealth and power—and since she was my wife I actually had to listen to her. I still brought in a cleaning crew every month or so, because *I* sure as fuck wasn't going to clean every room of our two floor, *five bedroom* estate. We were barely home enough to do our laundry.

We had held our wedding ceremony several months after the angels moved in. It was an open-venue banquet at the Temple of Maghir in Moritoria, and twenty thousand people attended. We hadn't had much then, Sanctum's reconstruction still in full swing, but we'd ordered as much food as we could and our guests had danced all night.

The rest of my day was filled with meetings. Not much had changed there, but my job was a lot easier now that Sanctum wasn't in a permanent state of collapse. Our city was flourishing, and (grudgingly) I had the angels to thank for that.

At half-past three, Ara found me at the coffee area in the lobby. He worked two floors down, now head of the Department of Law and Defense. The Sanctum Militia and its Enforcers division dissolved three years ago, and I'd combined what was left with our law enforcement department. No need for a giant army anymore.

"Regent," he greeted, pouring himself a cup.

"Commandant."

Ara had a look on his face that told me he was having a really bad day. Like me, he'd been yanked from a military position to a desk job, and wasn't transitioning well. His armor was replaced by a suit and tie, and the youthful vigor that once shined in his eyes was dulled by every day monotony. *Welcome to the club,* I'd said.

We stood aside as another group of suits approached the coffee stand, sipping ours quietly. They nodded to us, and we nodded back.

"Want to talk about it?" I asked.

"There's nothing to talk about. It's been too quiet lately. I'm so bored that I want to hang myself. Without impending doom, people act so stupidly."

"An example being…?"

"We just got a call for a domestic disturbance out in Central Sanctum. A woman was seen beating her boyfriend on the head with a frying pan."

I smiled.

"The most exciting part of my day was incarcerating the arsons who'd burned down that clothing store a week ago."

"You caught them?"

"One of the employees and her husband. The owner of the store failed to mention that he'd been sexually harassing a worker, and when she didn't reciprocate, he fired her. She came back with her husband and burned down his store that night. We arrested the arsons and the owner for malicious mayhem."

"Your day sounded better than mine."

"You get to talk to people about money. I talk to people about their reprehensible life choices."

I shrugged, having no counterargument. Ara tossed his empty cup into the waste bin. "Has Ila called Leid yet?"

"Don't know."

"She wants to set up a get-together with Tae and Roen this weekend at your house."

"At my house, of course. Never yours."

"Your house is bigger."

"I'll ask Leid when she gets home tonight."

Ara nodded, sighing. "Back to work. Only thirty-three minutes left of this crap."

I paid him a look of sympathy as he sulked off. My poor brother.

Tae and Ara had left Eroqam six years ago, both married and living in estates of their own. Tae had settled with a wealthy official named Roen Artuega, assistant Director of Commerce, and Ara with Ila Yema-Torin, eldest daughter of the owner of Yema Theater.

Life had swooped in and changed everything—a bittersweet factor of time and growth. Sanctum's war with the angels and my crusade to crush them all seemed like a distant memory, a vivid nightmare from long ago. Once upon a time I couldn't even imagine peace, and now I couldn't remember how life had been without it.

Sometimes I wished my father was still alive so that he could see how everything turned out. There were a lot of things that I regretted doing. *Too many things.* But hindsight only scarred your soul. The past never had anything new to say, so I wouldn't dwell in it.

***

"Qaira, your fingers."

"What about them?"

"They're stiff. Your notes are coming out flat."

I was a renowned violinist, but Leid never failed to keep me grounded. "Whatever."

"No, not whatever. The symphony is in two weeks."

I gestured to the two empty bottles of wine on our end table. "I'm finding it a little difficult to practice right now."

She grinned.

We spent the night playing music, our kitchen and dining room table still in chaos from dinner. Our house was always in a state of post-apocalypse, what with no maid and our mutual dislike of cleaning.

But I didn't care, and neither did she. We drank life like wine—thirsty, *passionate*.

Leid set her cello aside and pried the violin from my hands. I watched, confused, but not confused for long, as she slid into my lap. She had stripped to her undergarments after dinner, her skirt suit still in the middle of the dining room floor. She unfastened my belt and I leaned back.

"Let's sober you up," she proposed.

She lowered her head between my legs and I inhaled, clutching at the couch. Fellatio was a rare event.

I watched her head bob, feeling the warmth of her lips and the sharp yet enticing sensation of her teeth. Leid never dealt pleasure without pain, and I had learned to love it.

My breathing grew heavy and my stomach muscles tensed as she worked me over, worshipped me. But I refused to close my eyes and kept watching, transfixed. Sometimes I still found it hard to believe that all of this was real. A scholar had come to my world ten years ago, powerful, untamable, teeming with animosity for both me and my beliefs.

And now here she was, between my legs, forever wearing our vows. The ink shined across the smooth, pale flesh of her arms, like fresh scripture over bleached parchment. It was beautiful.

She was beautiful.

My arousal fueled her own, and in no time she was straddling me. After we were done, we resumed our places on the couch, instruments at the ready.

"Better?" she asked, still a little heavy-breathed. Our sex was never gentle. It was hard, and violent, and *savage*. The kind that left a stitch up your side and tremors in your legs. I was always covered in scratches and bite marks.

I nodded.

"Alright, let's take it from the top."

V

REVERIE

MY FAMILY WAS LAUGHING IN OUR DINING ROOM.

I was in the kitchen, shot-gunning Cardinal. The work week had been terrible and I couldn't pull myself out of this rut. Soberly, at least. Seldom did my brother and sister ever visit, and I wanted to be in a good mood for them. So, *bombs away.*

Fiercely abuzz, I returned to my seat with a jar of seasoning that I didn't really need—only used as an excuse to slip away—and rejoined their conversation. In my absence, the topic had switched to malay. Nothing like discussing work at home.

But it was inevitable, really. That was our city's only remaining blight. No one else knew about the clinical trials that Yahweh had proposed, except for Leid. Maybe several years from now malay wouldn't be the prime choice of every discussion. Until then, I was forced to hear about it over and over. *And over.*

"Drug incarcerations are on the rise again," said my brother. "And you wouldn't believe the people we've brought in on drug charges. Important people. People who would be ruined if anyone knew. Malay isn't just for the dredges."

I knew that better than anyone, and my secret still lived to this day.

"Really? I haven't heard anything about it in the headlines lately," said Tae. "I thought maybe it was getting better."

"No, it's only getting normal. If the press released every malay charge and overdose that we saw, our newspapers would be novels."

"That's a depressing thought," Roen muttered, sipping wine. "Didn't Ila have a friend who just got arrested for malay?"

Ila nodded, solemn. "Unet. Remember her, Ara?"

"Kind of. I remember her boyfriend more. What a dick."

"We went to school together. She was training to be a lia-dancer. She and her troupe performed at our theater three times last year. It's sad. Her life is ruined now."

I kept quiet, cutting up my steak.

"There might be some hope," Leid said, and I looked sharply at her.

"What hope?" asked Tae.

"The Plexus is—"

"Leid," I cut in, "that's supposed to be confidential."

She arched a brow. "Even to your siblings?"

Everyone at the table was staring at me. I sighed. "If any of you repeat what Leid is about to say, I will kill you. *Personally.*"

"And the most fucked up part about that is you're probably serious," said my brother.

All I did was wink.

Leid explained to them—in excruciating detail that took me back to those three insufferable hours in the conference room—all about Yahweh and the Plexus' invention of a malay-like drug. Everyone sat there with wide, sparkly eyes, soaking up the prospect of a miracle cure like a sponge.

… And that was why I hadn't wanted them to know. I didn't want to get anyone's hopes up. This wasn't the Plexus' first attempt at a cure for our malay epidemic. I'd actually lost count of their attempts.

When the topic ran out of steam, Tae announced that she was pregnant. Everyone was stunned.

"Congratulations," I said, and meant it. "You should probably stop drinking."

"I will after tonight," she said, laughing. "I'm not far enough along yet for a drink to hurt anything."

"When did you find out?" asked Ila.

"Last week. I wanted to wait and tell you all in person."

Roen smiled proudly, wrapping an arm around my sister. I didn't like him much—he had an air of snobbery, much like every other powerful suit in Sanctum's upper echelon, but he loved Tae and kept her safe, and that was all that mattered. She'd been charmed by his looks and sharp wit, and it wasn't too long after his courting that she'd agreed to marriage.

I hadn't found him nearly as endearing at first, especially the way his mouth quirked whenever he smiled, like he wasn't really smiling but just pretending to, along with that devilish look in his eyes whenever they held you. But he grew on me. I came to learn that Roen wasn't really an asshole; he just looked like one.

Ila was more than tolerable. Ara had certainly stepped up from his last catch. Few Nehelians were fair-haired, *fair* being auburn or sandy blonde, but she was, with kind brown eyes and tawny skin. She was smart and independent, and I had no idea how Ara had bagged her.

No offense to my brother, but they were nothing alike. Her affection couldn't have stemmed from his title or money either, because she'd already possessed both. Ara wasn't stupid but he held zero interest in art, meanwhile his wife was a dance instructor and curator of Yema Theater.

In any case, good for him.

"What about you, Qaira?" asked Roen, smirking. "Any children in your future?"

The table fell dead silent. My sister shot her husband an appalled look, while Leid lowered her gaze.

And then Roen's face filled with revelation. "*Oh*. I... I totally forgot. That was so rude of me, I'm sorry."

I glared at him, unable to tell whether or not he'd said that on purpose. That was another thing I didn't like about him. He was unreadable. I didn't want to believe that he'd just taken a stab at me. Roen didn't have a death wish. His embarrassment seemed genuine, too.

"Don't worry about it," I said, patting Leid's leg underneath the table.

"Take it as a compliment," Ila said, smiling uncomfortably. "We've all forgotten that you're not one of us."

"She *is* one of us," I said.

Everyone nodded their agreement, and Leid smiled.

"Thank you," she said. "You're very kind."

More silence.

"Soooo," Ara ventured, "has anyone noticed how cold it's been lately?"

***

I had totally forgotten about the work that I'd taken home with me, and now was forced to do it drunk. I had to squint to keep the numbers on the budget report from swirling around, and it took me twenty minutes to calculate something by simple arithmetic. But the weekend was over and this was due tomorrow. I wanted to be angry, but the only person I could be angry at was *me* since this was entirely my fault.

Leid had finished cleaning up the dining room and kitchen. Our guests were gone, and had been for an hour. She didn't have to go back to work for three weeks, as the academic period had ended and there was always a month break between a new one, but I should have been in bed a long time ago.

"Does it bother you?" I heard Leid ask from the dining room doorway.

"What?" I mumbled, juggling with her vague question and arithmetic.

"That we can't have children?"

I froze, looking at her. She looked back at me, leaning on the doorframe, sadness etched across her face.

"No," I said. "I knew that when I married you. That doesn't matter to me." But I was beginning to suspect that it mattered to her. Thoughts of Roen and his stupid remark stirred more anger. He'd just opened a box that wasn't easy to close. "Are you alright?"

"Yes," she said, moving to the chair beside the couch. Leid was small enough to fit her entire body in it and she curled, resting sideways with her head against the arm. There was a feline aspect to my wife. Sometimes she would curl like that across my lap, like an attention-depraved pet. It was weird and sexy all at once. "I take it you never wanted children?"

"I don't know. I never thought about it." And when I finally did, I wondered what that child's life would be like if he or she was given my curse. No one deserved that.

Leid yawned and stretched. "Are you almost done?"

"Nope."

"Due tomorrow?"

"I wouldn't be sitting here if it wasn't."

"Must you hand it over first thing in the morning?"

"Probably not," I said, suddenly knowing where this was going.

Leid smiled coyly and slipped out of the living room.

I sat there looking between my report and the hallway. And then I sighed in defeat and threw the report aside, following her.

Twenty minutes later I was glaring cross-eyed at the ceiling as Leid rode me into near-insanity. Her sexual appetite was appalling, in a good way, and her stamina was unreal. Trying not to come first was like trying to move a mountain. Impossible. *Hopeless.*

And she liked it that way.

Her fingernails dug harder into my chest and I clenched my teeth. She moaned and bucked and moaned and bucked and then my eyes rolled into my head as tingly warmth settled in my groin. My stomach tightened and I arched my back, warning Leid that I was dangerously close.

She slowed, keeping me on edge. Her hands left my chest and slid up toward my neck, fingers curling around my throat. She squeezed, lightly, but it was enough to labor my breath.

Her grip tightened and tightened until she was crushing my throat. Now I couldn't breathe at all and my eyes shot wide open. She was staring down at me with a wicked grin, eyes pitch-black.

Black eyes.

I lay paralyzed, suffocating, while she fucked me with abandon. I had no idea what was happening or why it was happening—memories of that event in the music room flooded back, where she had sung that morbid hymn. And then she'd cried, and her eyes had looked like *this*.

I had forgotten all about that. *It wasn't real,* I'd told myself.

She was too strong; I couldn't shove her off. I couldn't pry her hands from my neck either. Leid was killing me and all I could do was watch.

My vision blurred and that warmth in my groin returned, fiercer than ever. A gurgled choke escaped my lips as I exploded, and she rode me through it, whispering in my ear.

"That's it, that's it."

She licked the side of my face and laughed. I started to thrash—my air supply was getting fatally low—and our headboard slammed into the wall, fracturing the paint.

And then her grip loosened.

Cold air invaded my lungs and I threw her off. Leid tumbled from the bed and landed on the floor against the wall, back pressed against it with her knees to her chest. She hung her head, concealing her face in shadows.

I doubled over and coughed violently. My throat was bruised and raw, and a whistle accompanied each breath. She'd fucked me up pretty badly. I'd be lucky to swallow anything tomorrow.

Leid was still and silent, almost catatonic. I watched her silhouette from the bed, icy tingles of confusion and fear plummeting down my spine.

"Leid?" I rasped.

Nothing. Just the soft rattle of her breath.

I crawled to the edge of the bed, peering over it. I didn't call to her again, only watched and waited, though not entirely sure what I was waiting for.

And then her body jolted like she'd been roused from a nightmare, and her head shot up and she looked at me. Shock, *confusion.*

"Q-Qaira?" Leid stammered. "What happened? How did I ..." She looked around her. "How am I here?"

I said nothing, staring.

"Answer me," she begged, seeing the reprehension in my eyes. "What did I do? What did I do to you?"

Something was wrong with my wife. Something had been wrong with her for a long, long time. It wasn't something that I could fix, either. That I knew. Her problem was as alien as her, and only another scholar would have any answers.

"What's wrong with you?" I said. "Why does this keep happening?"

Leid looked away, shivering. "I don't know. I don't."

"You're going to call that a panic attack?"

"I'm sorry. I... I don't know why it happens. I don't know anything." She held her face, fighting tears. "I'm sorry. *I'm sorry.*"

Leid kept repeating that until I felt guilty for being afraid. I scooped her up and held her, *shhing* into her ear.

"Did I hurt you?" she whispered.

"No," I lied. She didn't need to know what she'd done. That wouldn't help anything. Leid would probably see the bruising on my neck tomorrow, but right now I didn't want to talk about it.

We curled into bed and I held her until she fell asleep.

I stayed awake all night, wondering what any of this meant.

VI
STRINGS, *TIGHT*

"THIS WILL BE THE DIAGNOSTICS AREA, AND the large room on your left will be the patient-living quarters."

Yahweh was pointing in two places at once, while Leid and I tried to follow him to no avail.

He had found a name for the malay-like drug—*Axium*—and all of its safety tests had passed. They'd fed doses of Axium to a dozen different animals over the course of a few weeks, and none of them had shown any harmful side-effects. Aside from being stoned.

We had arrived at the Plexus an hour ago. It straddled the border between Moritoria and *Heaven*—the angels' two-layer territory.

The Plexus was an enormous glass sphere that floated atop the Areva Sea, The Atrium's largest body of freshwater. The few times that I'd been here, I marveled at it from the window as our craft approached the tunnel port. The top of the structure reflected the sky, and the bottom reflected the water. It took on a two-tone iridescence, like a beacon against Moritoria's bleakness.

The Plexus' interior was blinding. Everything was *white*—walls, furniture, even the scientists' uniforms. Spending more than two hours here always gave me a skull-splitting migraine. This time I brought sunglasses.

The new wing was nearly complete, and Yahweh had scheduled to show us around and discuss the possibility of an Axium clinical trial. It was strange that he held such enthusiasm toward helping a city that had otherwise shunned his people, but then again Yahweh didn't operate on charity. He operated on work—title, claim, *greatness*. If malay was cured, he would take the credit. Just another achievement to stuff under his child-size belt.

Yahweh reached into a folder and retrieved a document. He handed it to Leid. "Here is the procedure for the trials. We're going to need at least one hundred and fifty addicts. Seventy-five for the experimental group, seventy-five for the control."

I had a hard time believing that *any* Nehelian would volunteer to play lab rat for a group of angels.

"Looks sound," said Leid, glancing over the procedure.

Yahweh beamed. Seldom did she give him a perfect score. "The next step is gathering our test subjects. I would recommend a televised advertisement."

"I have a better idea," I said, recalling Ara's complaints at dinner. "There are over five hundred Nehelians awaiting trial at Perula's Peak for malay possession. I can have Ara offer to drop their charges if they agree to participate in your clinical trial."

Yahweh looked at me as if I'd just solved the mysteries of the universe. "That's... a wonderful idea."

"You're acting like I never have any good ideas."

He gave me a nervous laugh and changed the subject. "I'll let Commander Raith know that we've been cleared to proceed. When do you think you'll talk to your brother?"

"Later today. I'll call you and let you know what he says."

"Perfect."

"Are we done here? I have another appointment in an hour and I haven't eaten lunch yet."

"I can't think of anything else. I'll call the driver and let him know that you're ready to leave."

Yahweh nodded to both of us and headed for his office. As Leid and I made our way to the port, I remembered something.

"There's something I forgot to ask him," I said. "Can you run ahead and wait with the driver so he doesn't think we're lost?"

"Sure," she said.

Leid continued on without me and I watched until she disappeared behind the closing elevator doors. When she was gone, I hurried over to Yahweh's office.

"Hey," I said, not bothering to knock. The kid had his back turned and at the sound of my voice he jumped, dropping a cluster of files at his feet.

"Goodness," he mumbled, kneeling to collect them. "You nearly gave me a heart attack."

"Sorry. Can I ask you a question?"

"Depends on the question."

Yahweh's face deadpanned as I shut the door. He'd realized it was going to be *that* kind of question.

"How much do you know about Vel'Haru?"

He hesitated. "Quite a bit, I guess."

Even though the door was shut and we were completely alone, I still looked over my shoulder, half expecting someone else to be there. "Have you ever heard of them checking out?"

"… Checking out?"

"Yeah, like going insane."

His face changed again, but it was imperceptible. "Can you be a little less vague?"

I wasn't about to tell the kid that Leid had almost choke-fucked me to death. "Do their eyes ever turn black? Do they ever… get violent?"

Yahweh stared at me, seeming a little disturbed. "I haven't ever heard of that happening, no. Is everything alright, Qaira?"

I looked away, trying to hide my disappointment. "Yeah, fine." And now this was really awkward. "Thanks anyway. I'll give you a call when I talk to Ara."

Before the kid could say anything else, I was gone. I'd seen him step into the hall in my peripherals, watching my departure. Yahweh had just stated that he didn't know what I was talking about, but his face said otherwise.

He'd looked scared, *grave*.

Telei wasn't telling me something. I should have forced it out of him, but couldn't here. *Not here.* I'd have to get him alone, and that would be easy enough to arrange.

***

My stool was uncomfortable and the murmuring crowd beyond the curtains wreaked havoc on my nerves. The bow kept sliding through my fingers because my palms were coated in sweat.

I'd performed twelve times before this, but it never got any easier. Stage fright was in my blood. Ironic that the Regent of Sanctum suffered crippling stage fright, but here I was, shaking like a lamb led out to slaughter.

My mother had been part of the Sanctum Symphony, and I'd continued her legacy. Once a month I played at Yema Theater for an audience that was sometimes as large as fourteen thousand. Tonight there were ten thousand.

Our conductor shouted for everyone to get into position, and musicians scrambled across the stage with their instruments and sheet-books. I was already in place, and so was Leid, sitting across the stage with the other cellists. She wore a violet dress and her hair was tied in a white ribbon. Beautiful, as always.

And she was never nervous.

"I hope I can hook that bridge this time," muttered Dhan, a violinist. He studied his sheets, a frown pulling at his lips.

"All about that quarter beat," I said, tightening my strings.

"It's not that. It's something about the way the trumpets come in. Throws me off every time and I start to follow them."

"Then you should play the trumpet."

Dhan rolled his eyes, and I grinned.

The lights dimmed; all of us fell silent, even the audience.

The curtains drew slowly and we were smothered by spotlights. All I could see was the stage and other musicians. The audience had become a sea of silhouettes, which soothed my nerves.

The conductor raised his wand, holding it there.

Drums.

We raised our violins, tucking them beneath our chin.

Cellos.

Then us, balancing the somber melody, adding a lighter texture. Music came in layers, levels. It was amazing how different the same song sounded, all depending on the instrument.

Our opening song was called *Truen di Abadena*. March for the Abandoned, an ancient hymn sung on the way to battle. A personal favorite.

We became a conglomeration of rhythm and strokes, each area moving differently, but it all seemed perfectly choreographed. Cameras flashed from the audience, and I wondered how many of them were taking pictures of me. Since the angels' settlement, my image had been transformed from Warlord to Humanitarian, and violinist for the Sanctum Symphony only added to that persona.

By the middle of the concert I was sweating like a pig. Between each song I had to wipe the coat of perspiration accumulating across my forehead and hands. The spotlights were slow-roasting us. Who knew that playing the violin could be such a workout?

And then something felt different. The air. *The gravity.*

My eyes swept over the crowd, still faceless shadows. All except for one.

A man was sitting front row center, radiating a spotlight of his own. He wore a white suit and purple tie, with jet black hair that spilled across his shoulders, reaching all the way to his ribs. He was handsome, almost surreally so, with sharp features and a soft mouth pulled into a curious frown.

Silver eyes. *No rings.*

Not Nehelian.

Not Nehelian, my mind repeated. I almost stopped playing, but forced myself to keep on. All the while we stared at each other, silver against silver, and there was ice where our eyes met.

I shot a glance at Leid, but she didn't see me, or him. Her head was down, eyes closed in fierce concentration. She always memorized our songs.

A Vel'Haru was here, watching us. Why? After ten years, why now?

I wanted to snatch my wife and flee, but I was stuck on this stool until the concert was over, giving that Vel'Haru plenty of time to plan.

My pulse was in my throat, and my stomach began to churn with unease.

But when I looked back at him, the chair was empty.

He was gone.

***

We had planned for drinks with Dhan and his wife after the concert, but I faked sick and canceled.

I didn't tell Leid about what I'd seen during the performance. I wasn't sure why, but for some reason it didn't seem right to tell her. Not yet.

Leid was waiting for me in the lobby. It was raining and I told her I'd bring our craft around since her dress had cost three hundred usos. The truth was that I wanted her to stay in a crowded area.

I hurried through the parking lot, shivering. My coat was already soaked and each breath left my lips as tiny plumes of steam. Cold season had begun several weeks ago, and pretty soon it would snow. I needed a thicker jacket.

I unlocked my craft and threw my violin case in the cabin. When I shut the door and turned around, I jumped.

That Vel'Haru was standing twenty feet away, leant against a median-pillar. When our eyes met, he smiled.

"Who are you?" I demanded.

"My name is Calenus Karim," he said.

Him.

Honestly, he wasn't what I'd expected. But Namah had been right again—nobles had a certain look to them. Calenus was... deific. Tall, taller than Commander Raith, with features that appeared chiseled from stone. Our eyes were identical, but his seemed to *glow*.

"You're a talented violinist," he said. "I enjoyed your performance very much."

"What do you want?"

"I want to turn around and go home," said Calenus, sadly. "But I can't. Not until I tell you something that will break your heart." Before I could respond, he looked back at the theater, the sadness on his face waning. "Leid seems happy here."

"She is."

"That's good. Another of us destroyed her life once, and when he died I tried to fix her. I knew I couldn't undo the damage, but I at least tried to make her happy. I failed, yet here she is, *happy*, and it's elating. And painstaking."

I said nothing, utterly confused. "So... *why* are you here again?"

Calenus looked back at me, the warmth in his expression gone. He was frigid. "She has to come back, Qaira."

Panic squeezed my chest and my heart began to race. "Ixiah promised me that she could stay here. The contract was voided. Leid was excommunicated from your court."

"My guardian made a deal with you that he had no power over. If I could keep his word, I would, but there is something that he doesn't know."

"Which is?"

He looked away, conflicted. "Leid is sick."

Sick. Calenus didn't even have to tell me what that meant. I already knew. "What happens to her? Why do her eyes turn black?"

"So you've seen it."

"Tell me what's wrong with Leid. Can you help her?"

"What she has isn't curable, and it progresses. Keeping her here will put your world at risk."

No.

No, this couldn't be happening. "She's my wife."

"I know. I know how you feel, but you have to understand that this isn't personal. I'm trying to save your world."

His cryptic explanation wasn't cutting it. I wasn't going to toss my wife back into the very nightmare from which we had almost died to free her. "Are you asking for my permission?"

"I need your permission. I can't force Leid to come back. If we fought here, it could ruin your city. You have to be the one to persuade her to return."

Calenus was asking me to break her heart. Turn her out, so she would have nowhere else to go. "Forget it."

I moved away, opening the driver-side door of my craft, cueing that our conversation was over.

"If you don't listen to me now, the next time we meet it'll be too late."

I said nothing and shut the door. When I searched for him through the window, he was gone—

And then he was *right* in front of my craft, clearing a twenty foot distance in a second flat.

"Listen, *please*." Even though I shouldn't have been able to hear him, Calenus' voice rang clear as if he was sitting in the passenger seat. "You have to let her go. Your world will collapse if you don't."

"Quit with the melodrama," I snarled. "If Leid was putting our world at risk, she would have already left."

"She doesn't know."

It was true. She could never remember her episodes. Could I tell her? *Should I?* If I did, she might leave, and I didn't want her to leave. I didn't want her to know. And for some reason, neither did Calenus.

None of this seemed right, and my suspicions were growing stronger by the second.

I started the ignition. "Get out of my way."

Instead of complying, he placed his right hand on the nose of my craft. "Her eyes turn black whenever she loses herself. There is something inside of her—something *else*. That something does not love you, or anyone, or *anything*."

"I said get out of my way!"

"It feeds on weakness, eating little pieces of her at a time. Soon Leid won't be able to keep it down and it will take over completely. And then you'll die. And then your world will die. Everything it touches will die, until the Multiverse is gone."

Fine, fuck him.

I floored the pedal.

But the craft didn't budge. Calenus was holding it in place with *one* hand.

His lips twisted into a snarl. Obviously he was not too pleased with the fact that I'd just tried to run him over, and the look in his eyes relayed that I had about five seconds before he killed me.

I reached into the glove box and ripped out my gun, firing through the windshield. Glass exploded everywhere, raining across my face and lap, and then suddenly my craft lurched and barreled forward at the speed of light. I stomped the brakes and my craft came to a screeching halt at the other side of the lot, only several inches from a guardrail.

At first I just sat there, breathing heavy. My eyes darted to each window and mirror, but Calenus had disappeared again, this time for good.

I didn't believe that I'd fatally wounded him. Or even tickled him. The noise from my gun and shattering windshield probably attracted more attention than he'd liked. Specifically the police craft that was making its rounds around the theater.

Even more specifically, *Leid.*

"Qaira?" she shouted, running toward me. The cello case in her hand might as well have been a sheet of paper. "What happened? Are you alright?"

No, I was not alright. I was soaked and shivering, looking around my craft as if a monster was about to leap out of the shadows and drag me off. "I told you to wait for me in the lobby."

"I heard shots fired." She didn't seem to know what had happened, which meant she hadn't seen Calenus.

Tell her, screamed my conscience. But I couldn't. It was clear that our life together was coming to an end, and if I said anything it would be over even sooner. I wanted to hold on to it—to her—for as long as I could.

Stupid and selfish, I know.

"Two men just tried to steal my craft."

Leid looked around, hand against her chest. "They got away?"

"I shot at them but they flew off. I might have hit one, though."

She looked back at me, and I couldn't read her expression. There was something in her eyes, like she knew I was lying. The rain had saturated her hair and it clung to the sides of her face. I could see her black lace bra through her sopping dress. "Are you hurt?"

"No, thankfully. Come inside before you get cold."

She did, and without another word I sped off. All Leid did was look out the window as shadows played across her face, casting dark lines that emphasized her concern. The whole way home I thought about her hands around my neck and those gleaming black eyes. I hadn't seen that in ten years. How long until I'd see it again? Ten years was long enough to forget, move on, and continue our life.

But I knew, *deep down*, that I would never forget, and nothing would ever be the same.

VII
OUT OF THE BLUE

"WE'VE REACHED THE LOWEST LAYER OF THE ATRIUM,"
Lucifer announced this morning over an Aeon bridge call. *"Our
crew says we have to see the mines."*

He had transferred over a blurry video recording that the
mining crew had taken of a cavern. The walls were covered in blue
glass, but its phosphorescence was like a strobe light, blinking at
three second intervals. Everyone was baffled and excited,
especially Lucifer, who had wanted to see that place for himself.

And now here I was, three hours later, sitting in a deep-
excavation craft that descended through the sixth-layer. Four
guards—two Nehelians, two angels—sat quietly in the cabin as
Lucifer and I traversed the freezing cold unknown.

It was the first time that I'd ever been so deep, and without
lights we would have been immersed in complete darkness. Tiny
flecks of frozen moisture—I couldn't call it snow or rain, sort of a
combination of both—hit the windshield, falling thereafter to an
endless sprawl of solid black tundra. It was unlivable here; the
scenery was a testament to that.

"How much further?" I mumbled, eyes glued to the window. I
hadn't said much because I didn't want anyone knowing how
terrified I was. Even though Lucifer and his crew had assured me

that their advanced technology would keep us safe, I couldn't help but feel like we didn't belong here.

And we *didn't* belong here. We were defying the elements that strived to keep us away for a good reason. If anything—even the littlest thing— went wrong, we all would die.

But that was a risk of progress, said Lucifer. He had spent half of our trip describing their deep sea excavations on Felor, and all of the incredible creatures and resources that they had found at the bottom of their oceans. All the while I'd sat there trying to program my headset. Archaean technology was a puzzle.

At the heart of The Atrium was a gaseous ocean, with islands suspended above it. The islands were layered—hence their name— and each was like a step up a ladder, all the way to Heaven. Tears in the layers allowed for deeper travel, but the pockets were located in specific places. We were coming up on the sixth layer's pocket now.

One of our engineers sent a radio transmission to the awaiting miners, letting them know we were half an hour out. They responded with directions to the cavern, but as the scenery grew even *darker*, I really had no idea how we were going to find anything. Lucifer and his angel scientists didn't seem too worried, though.

"External temperature has dropped to negative one hundred quasens. Wind speed is forty-five certas," announced some kind of scientist, seated at the systems control panel.

"Negative one hundred quasens," said Yahweh, whistling quietly under his breath. "Stick your hand out of the craft and it will freeze instantly."

Dr. Telei was here too, of course. He would never miss the chance of being part of a ground-breaking discovery. The kid hadn't said much since we'd left, only sat in a rolling chair and watched videos of the cavern. He kept freezing the footage and putting his face inches from the screen, as if that would help him see any better.

Fat chance. It looked like the camera man was having a seizure.

"I bet it's bacteria," Yahweh kept mumbling. "It has to be bacteria."

Why was I even here?

"I'm doing you a favor," Lucifer had said the moment I'd protested coming along. "Sanctum will want a claim in this."

The only upside to being here was that I'd had to cancel a meeting with the Board of Commerce. *Hooray.*

The craft groaned as it fought shell warping, pressure tremors shooting through the cabin. I sat upright, clutching my headset so tightly that it almost snapped.

"Reducing pressure," called the same scientist at the system control station. "Pressure decreased to seventy percent."

My ears popped, as did everyone else's, and we all spent a minute or two rubbing them.

There were several Nehelian scientists at the back of the cabin who were calibrating their drilling equipment. Yahweh had brought them from the Plexus. Other than that, I was sorely outnumbered. My guards seemed a little uncomfortable by this, too. Eighty percent of Sanctum still didn't speak Archaean.

Our craft was skirting another tundra, its lights sweeping across glacial terrain. The ice wasn't white, but blue. Sky blue, like we were flying over an endless bed of broken glass. We slowed at a giant crater and hovered over the mouth. Slowly, we descended.

Absolute darkness.

The craft groaned again.

"Pressure reduced to fifty."

I felt like vomiting.

"Suit up," ordered Lucifer. "We're ten minutes out."

Leid should have been here in my place. She'd have appreciated it way more than me.

We all changed into our thermal suits—skin-tight gray, supposedly flexible but really as stiff as rubber, and then an angel scientist had to help me with the headpiece. I still couldn't figure out its programming.

The craft wound through tunnels of blue crystal, tiny flecks of sparkling dust illuminating our windshield, casting out the darkness. It looked surreal; another world below the tundra. Still cold, but at least I could see now.

There was a mic and tiny speaker embedded into the headpieces of our suits, and Raith, Yahweh and the other scientists all chatted about procedural stuff. Another group was rolling the giant drill toward the ramp. Meanwhile I stared out the window, marveling at how my visor made our scenery crisp and *freakishly* clear, like I'd suddenly grown a set of high-res cameras for eyes.

The craft came to a stop when the cavern opened into a network of tunnels. There were four other crafts parked off to the side, their passengers suited and already outside. Field study machinery was scattered all over the place—wires and probes and strange geographic thermometer looking things. A group of suited angels were hammering something into the north-side wall. It was square and flashed data on a tiny screen.

The ramp lowered and we exited down it, followed by the group pushing the drill. Another group came to meet us, placing their hands to their chests in a salute to their Commander.

"Sir," the one in the center said.

"What have you got so far?" asked Raith.

"The light is photoelectric, but it's not radioactive. The cavern's temperature is negative four quasens. That's a ninety-eight quasen difference from topside."

"It gives off quite a bit of heat then."

"Yes, sir."

"Where is it?" asked Yahweh.

The scientist pointed down a narrow tunnel leading south. "Come, I'll show you the way."

Yahweh waved at the poor assholes lugging the drill to follow us.

The heat was prevalent before the phenomenon. Our suits recorded a spike in temperature—now almost survivable—and then a soft blue light filled the passage. It flashed in intervals, some kind of unspoken code, and each time the light came with a strange chime, like the soft jingle of bells.

The passage opened into yet another network of tunnels. It seemed very easy to get lost down here. The left wall was shimmering blue. The light faded, and then the right wall shimmered blue. Then the north, then the south.

We circled in place, watching.

Yahweh was the first to reach out and touch the wall's surface, tilting his head as it illuminated his glove. "It seems they're communicating."

I arched a brow, even though no one could see it. "The walls?"

"Whatever is inside the walls. This isn't an inorganic phenomenon. I'm thinking microorganisms, *bacteria*."

"Yes, we all heard you. A dozen times."

"Could bacteria communicate with each other like that? I've never seen it," commented one of the scientists.

"True, but then again this is a different world than the one we're familiar with," said Yahweh.

I'd grown brave enough to approach the wall, too. When it flashed, I caught a glimpse of how thin it really was. No denser than a sheet of glass. It flashed again, and this time I saw through it. Another tunnel.

"Hey," I called, *"look."*

The others huddled around me.

Lucifer stepped aside and pointed at the wall. "Drill."

"We're sure there's no radiation?" Yahweh asked.

"We're sure. We did the readings this morning," confirmed the scientist.

We all stepped back as the assistants pushed the drill up to the wall. It was the size of a cannon. Overkill much?

It whirred and screeched until a perfect circle was carved and fell to the ground. Yahweh bent over and picked it up, holding it to his visor. Behind him the wall glowed again, but this time the entire hidden passage was filled with soft blue light.

"It's not in the ice," said Yahweh, disappointed. "Something else is making that light." He held out the piece to one of his drill jockeys. "Can you take a reading of this? I want to know if there are any microorganisms in it."

The scientist took the piece and sauntered off, and then we all stood there, looking down the passage. Everyone kept glancing at each other, as if saying, *"You first."*

I stepped through. Might as well do my part.

As we slowly crept through the tunnel, I turned to Raith. "Remind me why I'm here again?"

"Energy."

"What?"

"If we can find the source of that light, we might be able to harvest it."

"Instead of nuclear power," I said, finally catching his drift.

"Exactly. Can you imagine the money and energy we could save if we found a natural way to generate heat and light?"

"No, but I definitely *want* to."

He laughed and hit me on the back. That caught me by surprise; he'd never touched me before. "You've got a bit of angel in you after all."

I was about to heatedly object but another ray of light swept across the tunnel, blinding us. The warmth that came with it spiked the temperature gauges on the lower right side of our visors.

"We're close," Yahweh announced, speeding up.

"Slow down," I said, grabbing his shoulder. "Stay behind us."

"Why?"

"It could be dangerous."

"Stop treating me like a child, Qaira."

"Says the child."

Yahweh huffed.

"Relax. I'm trying to protect you."

"Yes, I know," he muttered. "Thank you kindly for your concern."

The end of the passage was up ahead, blue light filtering through it in an endless stream, *veil-like*. I slowed in response, not entirely sure that I wanted to be the first to take *that* leap. The others slowed as well. We stood at the mouth, unable to see through it. Whatever lay beyond the passage was a foggy haze.

"Still no radiation," offered Yahweh, but he didn't budge.

"Hmm," pondered Lucifer.

When no one said anything else, I sighed and stuck my arm through the opening. Nothing happened. "Well, it won't kill us."

Together, we stepped out.

Tides.

We were on a shore. *The* shore. The fog was fumes of gas that seeped from the cloudy blue water, so blue that it shined. That was what we'd been seeing all along. The shore wasn't sand but mounds of fine crystal grains, violet in hue that glittered like stardust.

My people had always known there was an ocean at the heart of The Atrium, but no one had ever seen it until now. It was what had inspired the mythos of Maghir. Everyone was going to be extremely disappointed to hear that there weren't any black, festering waters filled with carrion. What would our priests do then?

As I stood there worrying about the religious/political inflections of our discovery, Yahweh inspected the passage mouth. He kept looking back and forth between the shore and the cave. Lucifer and his scientists were collecting some of the gaseous ocean water at the shoreline, being careful not to get any of it on their suits.

"Bioluminescence," he said aloud.

Everyone looked at him.

"Yahweh was right. They're extremobacteria." He held up the jar, shaking it. The intensity of the light grew two-fold. "They live in this ocean and their light generates heat. This is *ground-breaking*. If we could culture them, then—"

"How is this cave system here?" Yahweh interrupted, not even noticing that Lucifer had just given him all the credit.

"What?" I asked.

"This cave system. How is it here? If there are no microorganisms in the ice, how was it carved?"

"Heat?" said Lucifer.

Yahweh shook his head. "Can't be. Look at the mouth; it's a perfect semi-circle."

65

As revelation slowly crept in, the tides were broken by the sounds of splashes. Little ones at first, but then *big* ones that made us all turn toward the shore. We were just in time to watch a group of sticks break the ocean's surface—eight of them, arranged in a triangle.

No, not sticks. *Tails.*

They swayed and snapped, their tips as sharp as spears. None of us knew what to do, torn between running for our lives or watching what would happen next.

As they headed for the shoreline, Lucifer and the scientists backed away. More tails emerged behind them, now numbering twelve in total. Each was sectioned, dark blue and crystalline-looking. Every sway brought chimes.

Chimes. The sound we'd heard in the cavern.

The first line came ashore. Tails attached to six pincer-like legs, a body bearing some resemblance to a scorpion, and a bulbous head that flickered blue light. Each was as big as our craft.

Yahweh had received his answer. The cavern was a hive.

And then we were sprinting up the shore and through the passage, the sounds of skittering feet close on our heels. We would have been much faster by flight, but here our wings would freeze the moment we released them. Our suits did not make for easy running, either.

The kid wasn't nearly as quick as the rest of us, so I snatched him up and slung him over my shoulder. He was given an excellent view of our pursuers and started to scream.

Lucifer shouted orders over the radio to his awaiting team. *Prepare for immediate departure. Gather everything you can. Arm yourselves.*

None of us had expected this, therefore none of us were armed. Not even me. The one time that I decide to forego a weapon, we get hunted by monsters. Go figure.

"Let me take this opportunity to thank you for bringing me along!" I exclaimed, to which Lucifer didn't respond.

It was a two mile hike back to where we'd parked, and I was beginning to feel the effects of a decade-long desk job. My legs were aching and I couldn't catch my breath. Not even adrenaline was keeping up my stamina. Carrying Yahweh wasn't helping matters any.

Cracks erupted behind us like thunder. Pieces of the cave wall fell away as more creatures joined the hunt. The tunnels flashed blue, and now we knew what that phenomenon really was. Monsters lurking in the walls, talking to each other, studying us. Apparently they'd decided we were edible. At any second I was expecting them to surround us, but we were able to zip by quickly enough before that happened.

We exploded through the fork, the rumble of engines and glare of headlights flooded the passage. Scientists and guards alike stood in front of our crafts in rows, clutching temperature-resistant pulsar rifles. Those weapons could collapse the entire cave system, but being buried alive trumped being lunch.

Our group split to either side of the tunnel walls, out of their direct line of fire. The monsters erupted into the fork behind us, a raging tsunami of black and blue phosphorescence. There were dozens of them now.

That sight took our team by surprise. Only a few opened fire, the others—mostly scientists—watched, completely stunned. The ramp lowered and I tossed Yahweh (who was still screaming) to Raith. As our engineers prepared for departure, I cast a guilty look out the windshield as our team blasted away at the monsters, yet to no avail. They wouldn't last another minute. My guards were out there, too.

And I wasn't about to run off and let anyone die for me. That was never my style.

I swiped a rifle from the rack and flipped the CHARGE PRISM switch, ordering the angels to open the doors.

Lucifer didn't like my idea. "Qaira, no. You're the *Regent* of *Sanctum!*"

"Maybe you should have thought about that in the first place!" I snapped. "You want to run off and leave your people here to die, go ahead. I won't, so you better open that fucking door!"

I'd done two things just then. First, I made it known that even though I was Nehelian, I was still willing to protect angels. Second, I made Lucifer look like a coward.

After a second of heavy reflection, Raith grabbed a rifle as well. "Open that door."

***

"*Come to the mines,* he said. *It'll be sooo rewarding,* he said."

"I don't need your commentary."

"*Sanctum will want a claim in this*, he said."

We were en route back to Sanctum, ascending through the third layer, covered in scorpion guts. The larger part of our return flight was spent in the sanitization chamber, and now we were gingerly removing our suits, careful not to get any of that acrid-smelling crap on our clothes.

Yahweh had returned to the rolling chair, watching footage of our attack. Lucifer and I secluded ourselves at the back of the cabin, sorting out our shit. We had lost a craft, ten scientists, five guards and some really expensive equipment.

"Look at that," Yahweh said, pointing at the screen. "They're retreating *together*, displaying a kind of hive-intellect. The way in which they communicate is so puzzling."

We ignored him.

Lucifer reclined on the bench across from mine, his face creased with worry and fatigue. That fight hadn't been an easy one, and I was still a little surprised that we had even made it out alive.

"What are you going to tell your people?" I asked.

"The truth."

"That the mines we'd thought were so promising turned out to be a nest of deadly scorpion-ants?"

Lucifer tied back his matted, sweat-drenched hair. "I guess so. But it wasn't all for nothing, Qaira."

"No?"

"The extremobacteria could prove invaluable."

"How exactly are we supposed to get any?"

Raith's eyes left mine, and he frowned out the window. "I'll dispatch a team of seasoned soldiers to clean out that hive."

"We don't know if there are any more hives," interjected Yahweh.

Lucifer glanced at him. "And?"

"We could be killing off the only sub-layer multicellular species there is. When we came here, we all made a promise not to treat this planet like Felor."

He hesitated, thinking heavily on that. "You're right. We'll find another way, then. Maybe there's another route to the ocean."

Yahweh nodded, satisfied with that answer, and returned his attention to the video footage. "Although I wouldn't be opposed to collecting a live sample of one of those creatures. For phylogenetic purposes, of course."

Lucifer laughed softly, and I blinked.

"What did he just say?"

"Nothing, don't worry. I think he's trying to tell me that he wants a pet."

The subsequent minutes swept past in silence. I spent the time studying the angels' mini-pulsar cannons, marveling at the way the gas-core cylindrical chamber filled with smoke and blue lightning every time it charged. We had learned so much in the short decade that they'd been here. Our city was on the technological rise, all thanks to Heaven and the Plexus.

But there was still something gnawing away at me.

"What happened to Felor?" I asked. That question was one I'd always wanted to ask, but could never find the right time.

And it seemed that Lucifer was anticipating it. His face grew sullen, and it was a long while before he replied, "Her people were careless, drunk with prosperity. We didn't see the damage until it was too late."

Yahweh listened to our conversation, saying nothing.

"We sucked her resources dry, and even tore a hole in her sky. The old Commander, Raziel Denzas, ordered us to investigate quantum mechanics. Teleportation, to be exact. He had... become obsessed with trying to figure out how the Vel'Haru did things."

69

"Vel'Haru?" I repeated.

"Yes. He contracted a scholar to teach us the ways of quantum leap, but our request was denied. The Court of Enigmus said we weren't ready to tackle something like that. And they were right.

"But Raziel didn't take no for an answer, and instead sought the information elsewhere. Hasty, sloppy decisions were made. We ended up ruining our magnetic and gravitational fields. Felor was knocked out of her axial rotation and…"

Lucifer trailed off, but he didn't need to say anymore.

"Raziel was impeached and forced to go down with his ship. I rose to power and we left Felor on the Ark with as many angels as it could carry. And now here we are."

"You sound guilty."

"I am guilty."

"It wasn't you who ordered your world's destruction."

"No, but I was Raziel's first general. I had the power to stop it, and I didn't."

I shrugged and looked away, having no counterargument. Yahweh was pretending to watch the video again, but his gaze was empty, faraway. Felor was a sore topic, undeniably.

"Thank you for coming today," said Raith, smiling, or at least trying to. "Our discovery might have taken a turn for the worse without you."

He held out his hand, and I took it. It was the first time that we'd ever shaken hands. As we did, my gaze lowered to the metal prosthetic that had taken residence atop his right wrist. The memory of our near-fatal altercation on the Ark flickered through my mind, and for the first time—this was a moment for *many* firsts, apparently—I felt guilty for maiming him. Yahweh had been right. I hadn't known him. I hadn't let myself know him.

A light flashed and we both turned, startled.

Yahweh held a camera, beaming. "Sorry, had to. I doubt that will ever happen again."

VIII
PENANCE

MY SISTER AND I WERE JOGGING THROUGH the Eroqam Medical Facility port.

Roen couldn't leave his office to take Tae to her quarter-annual check-up. She had called me half an hour ago, and seeing as there was no one else and Tae *refused* to learn how to drive, I was forced to leave in the middle of a meeting, stating I had a family emergency. Which was kind of true.

We were ten minutes late, and the whole way Tae had mumbled about how they were going to reschedule and she wouldn't see a doctor for another month. I really had to bite my tongue or else I would have told her to learn how to drive and handle her own shit.

But she was my sister, and I loved her. She'd done a thousand things for me and Ara growing up, and this measured as only a tiny fraction of our debt.

The waiting room was vacant—it was noon-thirty in the middle of the work week—and thankfully the doctor was free. I had a feeling he was still free only because *I* was standing at the reception desk. But hey, whatever worked.

The attendant asked if I wanted to sit in, and I politely declined, not particularly keen on watching someone probe at my sister's snatch.

As the minutes ticked away, I sat on a chair near the ward entrance, staring vacantly at the wall. My portable Aeon kept chiming with messages from my secretary about meetings this afternoon, but I ignored them. They could wait. There was another message from Leid, ordering me to put dinner in the oven at six, to which I responded *'sure'* while making a gesture of shooting myself in the head.

The waiting room door opened and two small children, accompanied by their very pregnant mother, strolled inside. After checking in, they sat across the room. I tried not to make eye contact.

The kids immediately attacked the stack of magazines resting on a table. The little girl paraded around the room, wearing one as a hat. She marched by, looked at me, *stopped.* She stared and stared until I had no choice but to look back.

Her eyes got all big and she pointed. *"It's the Regent!"*

Someone kill me.

"Mommy, it's the Regent!"

I tried to smile, but it probably came out as a cringe. Children made me nervous. I never knew how to act around them.

Their mother was sympathetic. "Yes, Nakha, that's the Regent. Come here and leave him be."

Nakha ignored her mother. "Will you marry me?"

I laughed. "Maybe when you're a little older."

The mother waddled over and pulled her daughter back to her seat, mouthing an apology. Nakha waved and blew me kisses, and I pretended to catch them. How cute and awkward.

I thought that was the end of it, but the mother asked, "I never thought I'd see you here. Is your wife...?"

"No, my sister."

It was public knowledge that my wife was not Nehelian, but we'd never mentioned the Court of Enigmus. After years of speculation, the priests had finalized that Leid was an apostle of Maghir, given to us as a gift for our servitude. Everyone seemed fine with that answer, funnily enough. It was kind of scary how no one questioned anything pertaining to our spiritual beliefs. I was still young enough to evade any further speculation as to why we didn't have children, but that bridge was just down the road.

"Oh, congratulations."

"You, too," I said, nodding at her swollen stomach.

She smiled and patted her belly. "This will be my fourth. Maghir help me."

I smiled back, saying nothing.

Tae emerged through the ward entrance, and I stood to greet her. As we left, the children and their mother waved goodbye.

"Making friends?" Tae asked, smiling.

"You know me."

***

I didn't remember the port being so ominous.

Yet on the trip back to my craft, the silence was scary. The lot was practically desolate, peppered with a few empty crafts owned by medical staff. I should have parked closer to the entrance.

Calenus' visit two weeks ago had put me in a permanent state of paranoia. I walked through every isolated area with an eye over my shoulder, expecting him to pop out from behind each pillar, or around every corner. He had yet to return, but I knew that our ordeal wasn't over. It was only a matter of time before I'd see him again.

It was sleeting so I'd parked us under a port. Stupid move.

Footsteps.

A slamming door.

I spun, scanning the port.

Nothing. I was going crazy.

"Qaira, is everything alright?" asked Tae, sensing my unease.

"Yeah," I said, tugging her along. "Let's walk a little faster."

Now Tae was looking over her shoulder. "What's wrong? What are you looking at?"

Voices. Whispers.

No, I wasn't going crazy. We were being followed.

I stopped, shoving my sister behind me and pulling out my gun. Shadows of men stalked across the pillars, their silhouettes weaving in between the glare of overhead lights.

My sister was silent, understanding, and only clutched at my waist.

I waited for someone to step into clear sight, but instead I heard a *pop.*

Then, I felt a prick on the side of my neck.

I reached for it, feeling something cold and metallic protruding from my skin. I tore it out and looked at the tiny capsule in my hand. The sight was all too familiar.

A dart.

The dizziness was already coming on. I shoved my sister forward, shouting at her to run.

She did, and I only took two more steps before collapsing on my hands and knees, retching bile and fragments of breakfast.

The voices became louder, and Tae's cries turned to screams. There was a struggle happening ahead of me, and when I looked up someone's foot cracked the side of my head.

I'd caught a glimpse of men in enforcer masks, dragging my sister toward a revved craft, before my vision tunneled from the blow and I crumpled face down across the cement.

***

Cool air.

A dull roar.

Soft cries.

I opened my eyes, squinting against dim light. A migraine raged full throttle and even the shadows were too bright. I tried to stir but found that I couldn't move at all.

And then everything came flooding back, and my eyes opened wide, fear numbing the pain.

I was strapped to a metal chair, my wrists and legs bound in barbed wire. Little beads of blood trickled down my hands from my initial struggle, and my ankles stung, pant legs torn to shit.

The room was open and cold, aired by a noisy ventilation system that rattled somewhere in the darkness. Crumbled pillars marked with illicit art stood in rows around the room.

Lower Sanctum. An abandoned storehouse, maybe.

My sister was chained to one of the pillars, only several feet away. Her chains had some slack but she hugged the stone, sobbing quietly against it. There was a bruise forming at the side of her face and her dress was torn at the shoulders. Half of her hair had been ripped out of her braid, tangled and disheveled. She had put up a fight.

"Tae," I rasped.

At the sound of my voice she looked at me, hope and sorrow filling her eyes. "Qaira, I thought you were dead."

I didn't respond, surveying our surroundings. Whoever had put us here would be back soon, and I had to find a way out of this chair before then. Struggling was out, because even a minor yank could scrape the skin clean from my bones, and they made sure that I could not release my wings by compressing my back to the chair.

Once I realized that I was completely fucked, Tae caught a glimpse of the hopeless look on my face and began to cry again.

"Shh," I whispered. "Please, stay quiet. I need to think."

"What's happening?" she mumbled. "Why are we here?"

Those were excellent questions; none of which I could answer. Ten years ago there would have been a thousand reasons, but not now. Not anymore.

Enforcer masks. They had worn enforcer masks.

I didn't know whether they were soldiers or brutes trying to make a statement, and I could only speculate on their intent. They hadn't killed us outright, so perhaps this was a ransom attempt.

My vertigo sparked the memory of how they had subjugated me. That dart. *The sedative...* How had they known? The only ones who knew anything about that were—

The sound of a door opening put that thought on ice. Footsteps approached, numerous footsteps, and Tae hushed, making herself small against the pillar.

A group of men stepped from the shadows and into a patch of dim light, still wearing those enforcer masks. They lined up on my right, silent and still, acting like military. Tae and I watched, confused, *disturbed,* waiting for something to happen but almost a minute passed and they did nothing but stand there.

And then another set of footsteps penetrated the silence, this one less uniform than the rest. Erratic, excited—it almost sounded like skipping.

The line broke and another masked man emerged through it.

He wasn't skipping. There was something wrong with his left leg and he dragged his foot along the cement. A stool was resting by the pillar, one I hadn't noticed until now. The man snatched the stool and dragged it across the floor, along with his foot, producing a sound akin to nails on a chalkboard. I winced.

He set the stool in front of me and sat, placing his feet on the bar above the floor, hugging his knees. It was an odd position, like he was posing in a comical fashion.

"Good afternoon, Regent," he said with a minor tilt of his head. That gesture and his accent was enough for me to realize that he was not an enforcer or a dredge. He wasn't even Nehelian.

Confusion twisted my face, and he pulled off his mask.

Shaggy, platinum blond hair and light blue eyes—so blue they were almost white—with a mean grin that lifted only one side of his mouth. He was young, not too far past adolescence, and he wore a look that burned with absolution. This wasn't a ransom attempt.

How did he get into Sanctum?

How did he and the others get past border patrol?

How had he even *known* where I was?

Those questions overwhelmed me and I looked away.

He laughed. "Don't try to figure it out. You won't."

"What do you want?"

"That's a good question, Regent. *What do I want?*" He paused to scratch his chin. "I want my sister back, but that's something you can't give me."

When I only stared, he leaned forward. "My name is Micah Triev. Ten and a half years ago, you and your enforcers stormed our refugee camp and invaded my home. You assaulted my sister and when my parents tried to stop you, you killed them."

I remembered that.

His sister, *Ariel.*

"Can you imagine what it was like to come home and find everyone you love face down in a pool of blood? Shot dead and exposed in the street for everyone to see?"

"I didn't kill your parents."

"No, your men did. *Your* men."

"I punished the soldiers responsible. That wasn't my order."

Micah laughed again, but there was no mirth in his eyes. "You shot my sister in the back of the head while she was crawling away, screaming for help. *You.*"

"Your sister was covered in incendiaries and was holding one of my soldiers hostage. I tried to reason with her, but she wouldn't hear it. She was a rebel."

"That's where you're wrong, Regent. *I* was the rebel. Ariel was innocent. She found *my* weapons in our home and used them in self-defense."

I said nothing. I couldn't think of anything to say.

Micah turned and looked at my sister as she clutched the pillar, sniffling. She could hear everything that we were saying, and her knowing that I'd killed an innocent girl hurt me in ways no words could describe. Tae never knew how rotten I'd been.

"Let my sister go," I said, keeping an even voice, no matter how hard. "This has nothing to do with her."

"But this has *everything* to do with her. Look at you; your eyes hold no shame for what you've done."

My lip curled. "You don't know me."

His smile turned into a sneer. "All is well in The Atrium now. The angels and Nehel have found peace. But not me. I won't find any peace until we've shared the same experience. There is no torment quite like having your sister raped and beaten to death. But your punishment comes with interest; you get to *watch.*"

Tae screamed and yanked on her chains while our masked audience only watched her, still and silent as statues.

Hopelessness and terror coalesced. "Don't. *Please.*"

"I'm sure Ariel said the same thing."

"She's... she's with child."

The sneer on Micah's face waned and he looked back at my sister, conflicted. "Well... I suppose that makes this even sweeter."

"You fucking white!" I screamed, thrashing, ignoring the barbed wire shredding my wrists. *"I will hunt you down and rip out your fucking entrails!"*

Micah smiled, amused. "We'll see about that."

He nodded at his men, and they approached my screaming, sobbing sister, forming a semi-circle around her. One of them produced a knife.

They grabbed Tae by her braid and yanked her from the pillar, forcing her on hands and knees with the knife at her throat. She sobbed into the cement as they cut away her dress, exposing her breasts and wingslits.

I couldn't do anything to stop them. Tae was too close to use my ability. If I tried to hurt them, she would feel it, too.

Micah watched them touch her, sadness behind his gaze. "And this is where I take my leave. Brutality is a trigger. I'm sure you understand." He patted me on the shoulder and limped for the exit, receding into shadows.

One of them lifted Tae's right arm, grasping her tiny, trembling wrist in a monstrous fist. The one with the knife cut into her skin and she screamed again, louder and louder as they sawed through flesh, and then through bone. When done, they threw her severed hand aside and it landed inches from my feet.

I stared down at it, *numb.*

"Commander Raith sends his regards," said Micah, somewhere in the darkness.

Slam, went the door.

Those words repeated over and over in my mind as Tae knelt in a growing pool of her own blood. Our captors' hands had disappeared between her legs, but her stare stayed on me. She just kept looking at me with wide, disbelieving eyes as her skin paled and the fight in her faded.

    … And all I could do was watch.

O
TUMULT

Leid Koseling—;

"WHEN WAS THE LAST TIME THAT ANYONE saw them?" asked Roen, pale with worry.

Ara sat at our dining room table, his radio placed beside the stiff drink that I'd poured him an hour ago. Distorted discussions blipped through as soldiers and guards scoured the city for Sanctum's missing Regent and his sister.

My missing husband and sister-in-law.

"We found their craft abandoned at Eroqam Medical Facility," said Ara. "They were inside the facility at noon. That was the last time anyone saw them."

"That was eight hours ago. Where could they have gone?"

Ara had called my office this afternoon to inform me that Qaira and Tae were missing. He wasn't responding to any messages or taking any calls, and neither was Tae. Although Ara and Parliament were working diligently to keep their disappearances out of the headlines, it was getting very hard to lie to the press. Someone in Parliament must have told Sanctum PB, because the Aeon was chiming every other minute. None of us had answered it yet.

Roen and Ara were looking at me, waiting for me to shed some light on this. But I didn't have anything. I'd listened to their conversation for an hour, raking through memories that might offer a clue of what had happened. But I wasn't telepathic, or clairvoyant.

I was Vel'Haru, not omniscient.

But then I *did* remember something. "Qaira was attacked on Yema's port. Do you remember that? He said they were trying to steal his craft and he shot one of the perpetrators. You never found them, did you?"

Ara looked confused. "It's the first time I've heard about it. When did it happen?"

I hesitated, surprised. Qaira told me that he'd asked his brother the very next day to look into finding those craft-jackers.

He had lied. *Why?*

"Two weeks ago. The night of Sanctum's Symphony concert."

Ara shook his head. "He never told me about that."

Which meant Qaira was hiding something. I could safely bet that no one had tried to steal our craft that night. There was a struggle, shots fired, but...he'd looked so afraid. Qaira would have never been *that* afraid of petty criminals.

"Have you two been doing anything... questionable lately?" I asked, and Ara blanched.

"Define questionable," he said, narrowing his eyes. He looked so much like Qaira with that face.

"Questionable, as in *ten years ago* questionable."

"No," he said. "Never again. At least, not me."

Roen looked between us, curious yet self-restrained, knowing none of that was his business.

As if my inquiry came with a sprinkle of intuition, Ara reached for his radio. "Squadron Seventy, search the industry district in Lower Sanctum."

"Why there?" I asked.

He shrugged, but his eyes spun a different story. "Don't know. We haven't looked there yet."

Roen could no longer sit still and paced the dining room, fingers raking through his hair. "I can't believe this is happening," he muttered. "Do you really think they were kidnapped?"

Yes, I did, but who would be brave enough to kidnap Qaira Eltruan? And *succeed?*

"No one has called for ransom," Roen argued, sensing my answer.

"Sir, come in," said Ara's radio. He snatched it off the table.

"Go ahead, Sgt. Aruay."

"Some of the homeless just told us that they were driven out of their squat by a group of men in enforcer masks."

Ara looked at me, worry filling up his eyes. "When?"

"Sometime this afternoon. There were malay syringes on them so I don't know if their story is even true."

"Pretend it is and find their squat."

"Sir," another transmission interrupted the first. *"We've just received a call for noise disturbance by a bartender on Seventh. He said he heard screaming and gunshots from the abandoned grain storehouse across the street."*

Ara grabbed his coat. "I'm on my way. Get a team down there."

I grabbed my coat as well. He paused, questioningly.

"You might need my help," I said.

Ara thought about that, then nodded. We left Roen in the dining room.

"Shots fired?" he repeated, near tears. *"Screaming?"*

"Stay here," Ara said as we hurried for the door. "I'll call you the moment we know anything." Outside, he murmured, "We need to move quickly. I'm sure Sanctum PB has our radio tapped."

I nodded, keeping pace. When we reached the port, I climbed into the passenger seat of his craft, and Ara sped out of Eroqam. He looked more worried than I'd ever seen him, which did nothing for my panic.

"What has he done, Leid?" he whispered. "What has he done now?"

IX
LOST

WE WERE ALONE AGAIN.

The angels had stepped out of the room for a reason I couldn't fathom. But I wasn't trying to figure that out. I didn't even have enough strength to generate a cohesive thought.

Tae lay still and silent on the floor—face down, naked and bloody—but her shoulders heaved and I could hear soft, wet gurgles as her failing lungs still fought for breath.

I never stopped watching, even when it grew unbearable. Closing my eyes or turning my head would have been abandoning her. And so I'd suffered *with* her, until she'd no longer had the strength to keep her head up. If she was conscious now, I couldn't tell. I really wanted to believe that she was.

But a small part of me wished that she was dead, too. I didn't know if I could watch any more, and the thought of my sister having to endure another minute of this made my eyes wet.

I couldn't save her, and she knew that. She'd known that halfway through, when the last remnants of hope had faded from her eyes and she'd stopped fighting. Tae had just laid there and taken it, and I would never forget the way she looked at me.

Footsteps echoed softly in the darkness, but I kept my eyes ahead, thinking our captors had returned. There was an empty aching in the pit of my stomach, guilt and hopelessness savaging my insides. Surprisingly, there was no anger. There was nothing. *Nothing* could describe the way I felt as I listened to my sister die a slow, painful death.

A shadow emerged from behind a pillar, a silhouette of someone tall and lean. It didn't move for a minute, finally stepping into the light.

Calenus Karim.

He looked at me, and then at my sister laying several feet away. He wore an expression of confusion and sadness.

Passing Tae, he knelt in front of me and I looked him in the eyes, saying nothing. Calenus reached for my serrated restraints, snapping them away like brittle twigs. How he'd just broken metal was beyond me, but I didn't even question it. All I did was stare.

"It seems I came at a bad time," he said, softly. "Our conversation will have to wait."

And then he walked away, disappearing through the shadows. His silhouette seemed to disperse and meld with the darkness.

He'd freed me.

I was free.

The door opened with a *groan*, and the masked savages returned.

My eyes slid to their corners as they reappeared, one by one, into the flickering light.

O
BROKEN

Leid Koseling—;

PATROL CRAFTS AND GUARDS HAD THE ABANDONED storehouse surrounded.

Sanctum PB was already on the scene, but a group of Ara's men held them back at the parking lot. Sirens flashed through the cold darkness of the city's evening, and I watched our descent with trepidation. A lump had settled in my throat, persisting even when I swallowed.

When we landed, Ara pulled the keys from the ignition and looked out at the swarmed storehouse. I could hear his breathing, shallow and rapid.

"I hope this isn't him," he said.

I murmured a generic line of assurance, knowing that it was. It didn't take omniscience to gather that kind of intuition. My only hope was that Qaira and Tae were still alive. The lump in my throat was my conscience telling me that only fools hoped for things.

That thought made my eyes heavy, pressure building in my forehead.

No, don't cry. Not here. Can't scare the locals.

Together, we stepped out of the craft.

The crowd was a blur. Armed men stepped aside as we walked through the lot. Cameras flashed from the restricted zone— the media had seen us and were given enough fuel to spin a story—and we ducked, but it was too late.

A group of soldiers gathered around the sealed iron doors of the storehouse, readying a ram. Unnecessary. "Awaiting orders," said one, saluting Ara as he stepped into the shadows of the under-hang.

"Have you heard anything?" he asked.

"No, sir."

He motioned for them to move away, and then beckoned for me.

I stepped up to the door and pressed my ear against it. What I heard made my heart flutter.

Crying. Soft, whispered sobs.

I stepped back, squinting. "Someone's in there."

"Qaira?"

"I don't know. Someone. They're distressed." Ara pointed at the ram, but I caught his arm. "No, let me."

He glanced over his shoulder, making sure that we were out of public sight. "Go ahead."

The soldiers looked at each other, wondering what I was about to do. A moment later they gaped when I snapped the metal bolt that sealed the door and kicked it wide open. The door flew off the frame, adorning an indentation of my foot, and skidded away into the darkness. The air inside was hot, rancid from blood and sweat.

Ara and his men poured in, guns aimed at the shadows.

I stepped in after them, but everyone had frozen around the only working source of light. In front, Ara fell to his knees, hands against his head.

I broke through the crowd, freezing next to him.

There was Qaira, sitting on the floor cross-legged, surrounded by dead angels. Most of them were decapitated.

A chair wrapped in barbed wire lay on its side, next to a pillar twined with chains. They led to Tae, naked and lifeless, cradled in her brother's arms. Her hand was severed, wings ripped—not cut, but *ripped*—from her back, their loose black feathers floating atop pools of blood across the cement. Not a single patch of her skin was clean. She was a canvas of blue and purple bruises.

I covered my mouth, unable to stop the tears this time.

Qaira didn't even look at us. He stared ahead, vacantly, rocking Tae as tears streamed down his face. He was broken.

Everything was broken.

O
DANGER

Yahweh Telei—;

PAWN TO D4.

Bishop to C5.
Knight to C3.
I sighed, watching Lucifer snuff my rook.
He smiled. "Don't be so hasty."
Pawn to C5.
Bishop to G4.
Pawn to C8.
I took back my queen. "Check."
And as quickly as she came, she was murdered by a bishop. I wanted to cry.

"You're getting flustered," said Lucifer. "Take some time to think before you move."

It was hard to think because I'd gotten less than four hours of sleep in two days. Reports, tours, presentations… I needed to hire an assistant or twelve.

It was late in the evening and I should have been in bed, but Lucifer and I had little time to spend with each other during the day. These tiny night time get-togethers were all we could afford. So here we were, seated in his study, battling fatigue for a game of chess. A televised screen flashed current events on loop behind us

as we sat at a marble table, framed by bookshelves. The scent of
wicker hung in the air.

I had showered twenty minutes ago, towel still around my
neck. My hair was damp and this room was cooler than the rest of
our estate, making me shiver.

"You look really tired," Lucifer noted. "We should stop."

"In the middle of a game? That's sacrilege."

"What game?"

I frowned.

My ears pricked at the *beep* of an emergency report from the
televised screen. We were watching Heaven's channel, but Lucifer
had programmed our station to stream Sanctum's news as well,
displayed as scrolling headlines in a column at the side. He was
mostly interested in their economic news. But then my eyes caught
sight of one headline in particular:

ANGEL TERRORISTS KIDNAP REGENT AND HIS
SISTER. TAE ELTRUAN FOUND DEAD AT SCENE.

"W-What?" I stammered, watching the headline scroll to the
top, vanishing. I rubbed my eyes, wondering if I had imagined
seeing that. Surely that couldn't have—

But there it was again.

TAE ELTRUAN SLAIN IN LOWER SANCTUM AFTER
ANGEL TERRORIST ATTACK.

"Lucifer," I gasped.

He glanced at the screen, and then his eyes widened.

When that headline disappeared, too, Lucifer stood and
reached for the remote, honing in on Sanctum PB. The screen
switched to a live recording of an anchor in front of an industrial-
looking facility, sirens glaring behind her.

We listened to her story, neither of us uttering a single word.
When the live footage ended and a discussion started between two
other anchors at Sanctum PB headquarters, Lucifer shut off the
television. He sat there, stupefied, staring at the blank screen. So
did I.

Without another word, he left the table and hurried for the
door.

"Where are you going?" I called, starting after him.

"My office. Go to yours as well and check the status on each of your employees with *diplomatic* access."

I blinked. "Why?"

"I need to identify those brutes before Eroqam shows up on our doorstep."

Lucifer was right. It was only a matter of time before *grief* evanesced to *retribution*, and we would need answers at the ready.

But then I realized that Tae was dead, and I froze in the doorway. My legs felt wobbly and a wave of sadness overwhelmed me. Hand to my chest, I looked at the ground, knowing we would never share a laugh or cup of tea again.

Tae.

X
SPIRALING DOWNWARD

THE SOUND OF OUR ESTATE DOOR CLOSING SHOOK me from a fugue. Murmured voices grew louder as Leid and Yahweh appeared in the dining room, accompanied by several angel guards.

I sized up the guards, a little surprised that the kid had brought them. Maybe he was afraid of me.

Yahweh's eyes lingered on us, sadness etched across his face. I hadn't slept in three days and looked like complete shit. But sleep was impossible when every dream was a recount of Tae's death.

He noticed my stare on the guards icing over, and told them to stand in the hall while we spoke.

Everyone was a suspect, even the kid. Although I really doubted he had anything to do with this, people always had the tendency to surprise you. The guards, on the other hand, were prime suspects. They had diplomatic access and heard private conversations all the time. Without a doubt the masked murderers had been guards. As for Micah Triev…

"How are you?" whispered Yahweh, taking a seat across the table.

I didn't answer him. He already knew how I was. Instead my gaze lowered to the cup of tea, cold from neglect.

"Thank you for coming," said Ara, eyes searching the hall beyond. "Where's your father?"

"He… thought it was best not to come," said Yahweh, shifting nervously. "He assumed no one would want him here."

"Absence fortifies guilt."

"Absence fortifies self-preservation," said Yahweh, narrowing his eyes. It was a look I'd never seen, and it didn't suit him. "I'm here to clear his name."

"If Lucifer already thinks we're going to kill him, then I'd say you're off to a bad start."

Leid handed Yahweh a cup of steaming tea, and he nodded thanks. Ara reclined in his seat, crossing his arms. He waited for me to say something but I didn't, and so he led, "What do you have?"

Yahweh set a folder down on the table, pushing it toward Ara. "Take a look. That's everything we have on Micah Triev." As we opened it and sifted through its contents, he said, "He was hired at the Plexus seven months ago as a diaphoresis specimen processor. It was a Level One job."

"Level Ones have diplomatic statuses?" asked Leid.

Yahweh shook his head. "Only Level Fours. One of our Toxicologists reported his access badge stolen three days ago, the morning after Micah and his men kidnapped Qaira and Tae."

Ara set the folder down. "Where is he now?"

"We don't know. The badge was scanned at Heaven's border that night, and since then he's disappeared. Hasn't shown up to work, and his apartment in Crylle is empty. Our agents are hunting for him, though, so it's only a matter of time before he's found."

"When he is, I want Heaven to hand him over to Sanctum," said Ara. "He attacked our people, on *our* ground. We should be given prosecution rights."

"That isn't up to me," said Yahweh, sipping tea. "I'll make sure to ask Lucifer when I return to Crylle. But I'm fairly certain he won't have any problem with that." He glanced at me. "Do you remember what Micah looked like?"

"Why?"

That was the first thing I'd said in eight hours, and the sound of my own voice startled me.

"The only picture that we have to go on is one taken two hundred years ago when he boarded the Ark. He has no family, *obviously*, and we don't know who his contacts are. Level One scientists are not required to have picture-form identities to process specimens, so anything you can remember would be very helpful."

"You might want to change that procedure," said Leid.

Yahweh nodded. "We will. This won't ever happen again, I promise."

One time was too many.

But I couldn't remember Micah's face. Not entirely. Every time I thought back to that night, tried to recall its events, everything got fuzzy and my chest tightened up. The only thing I still remembered clearly was the way Tae had looked at me. The one thing I *wished* to forget.

Yahweh noticed my distress, looking sympathetic. "I'm sorry. I shouldn't have asked you that. We'll manage."

"He had a limp," I said. "That's all I can remember."

"A limp?"

"Yeah, he walked funny. One of his feet was messed up— turned in, I think. It looked like a birth defect rather than an injury."

"Thank you," he said.

Suddenly, the room got small. Yahweh was still saying something but I couldn't hear him and my vision tunneled. I sighed, trying to catch my breath, but the harder I tried the less I could breathe.

Leid sensed my unease and reached for me, but I could barely see her and instead I stood from the table and left the dining room without a word. I heard my name called several times as I hurried down the hall, but I didn't look back. I didn't stop.

I *couldn't* stop.

***

Yahweh found me at the port, half an hour later.

I was seated at a vacant dock, staring at the angel craft on the other side of the hangar. Yahweh's private vessel was revved and ready, Heaven-bound.

The guards dispersed and headed for the craft. He sat beside me, and for a while we didn't say anything—just stared into the darkness of the tunnel.

"Qaira, I'm so sorry," he whispered. "Words can't really express how sorry I am. Tae was a lovely, *lovely* woman and I'll miss her dearly."

Yahweh's apologies didn't move me. *"Commander Raith sends his regards."*

He looked at me. "What?"

"Micah Triev said that. His men cut off Tae's hand, and then he said that."

Yahweh only stared.

"He used that inhibitor dart to subjugate me. He knew enough about my ability to place Tae *exactly* within range."

"Qaira, I don't—"

"And Micah is missing without a trace? A nobody lab technician, without any recent photo identification, and none of you know what he looks like. That all sounds very convenient."

Yahweh's face twisted up. "Lucifer had nothing to do with this."

"How do you know that? You really think he'd tell *you?*"

"We were playing chess when we saw the news! He was just as shocked as me. You really think he would do something like that? *Really?*"

I didn't know. Three days ago, probably not. Brutality wasn't ever his bag, but all the pieces fit so well together. The only way Micah's plan had gone so perfectly was because he knew things about me that no one else did. Except for Lucifer and Yahweh. The kid was out, so that left one person.

"There are plenty of other ways he could have obtained that information."

"Oh?"

"He could have hacked the Plexus' private database."

I bristled. "Why would *that* information be in your database?"

Yahweh looked away.

"Hey, I'm talking to you. Why am I in your database?"

"Because you are able to explode people's heads on whim. That information is not public, but we've documented it because it's the most astonishing medical anomaly we've ever seen."

"And you have that sedative on there, too? What, in case I need to be put down?"

"Qaira, no. Calm down."

"*Calm down?* You've practically written a guide on how to destroy me!"

"It's not accessible to anyone."

"Except for that vendetta-fueled psycho!"

Yahweh sighed. "Fine, I concede. It was all my fault. I'll take down that information as soon as I get back to my office. But please believe that Lucifer had nothing to do with this."

"I want to see everything you have on me."

Now Yahweh bristled. "No, you can't."

"Why not?"

"Because…" he trailed off, fumbling for words

And then I remembered something. "What do you know about Leid's illness?"

Yahweh looked profoundly overwhelmed. "W-What?"

"When I asked you about Vel'Haru having black eyes, you said you'd never heard of that happening. That same night, Calenus Karim showed up at Yema Theater and demanded that I hand Leid over because she's *sick*. Tell me that's a coincidence."

At this point Yahweh had stopped speaking altogether. He didn't even try to feign surprise. All he did was look at me in tired defeat. Then, he lowered his eyes. "I'm sorry."

Yahweh left, heading for his craft.

I watched his departure, feeling my heart in my throat.

As the craft left the dock and drifted through the darkness, I stood and grabbed my radio.

"Ara, come in."

"Yes, Qaira?"

"Sanctum is closing its borders. Notify Air Patrol that we are no longer allowing any angels entry into our city."

It was as I suspected all along.

The whites couldn't be trusted.

XI
AT THE BOTTOM OF THE SPIRAL

"YOU SHOULD STOP AND THINK ABOUT THIS," said Leid, stirring her coffee.

I didn't respond, only fumbled with my tie. This morning marked my first day back to work. Sanctum needed its Regent, no matter if his sister died several days ago.

Although I'd made it very clear that my decision to close Sanctum's border wasn't up for discussion, Leid pressed anyway. "People are afraid. They're already talking about another war."

I sipped my coffee, watching the news. Tae's death still made headlines every hour or so, but it was finally fading. We refused to talk to the press about it and Ara warned Sanctum PB that I was not to be approached.

Tae's pyre was scheduled for tonight. It would only be the five of us—Ara, Ila, Leid, Roen and myself. Small and simple. *And private.* We'd burn her body after temple hours.

I tried not to think about it. I was still trying to cope with the fact that she was gone.

She was gone because of me; because of the things I'd done.

She was gone because I wasn't able to protect her when it really counted.

Sanctum's Savior.

Leid glanced at me after I'd laughed under my breath. I cleared my throat and grabbed my briefcase. "I have to go. What time will you be home tonight?"

She hesitated, concerned. "Are you sure you're alright? You don't have to go back today."

"Yes, I do. Things need to be tended to, meetings need to be held."

"And what of the angels?"

I narrowed my eyes. "What of them, Leid?"

"What are you going to do now that you've closed our borders?"

"I don't know."

"Do you have any idea what kind of message you're sending?"

I had a *perfect* idea. "I'll see you tonight."

I left our estate without another word, Leid's eyes burning on me all the way to the door.

***

Work was as I'd expected: *draining.*

There were a hundred condolence cards waiting in my mailbox. I took the stack and threw them in the trash as soon as I got in.

I spent lunch hyperventilating in my private bathroom, coaxing my reflection to get it together. I'd forgotten all about the picture of Tae and I taken on my birthday, resting on the table beside that ugly plant. One glance and my day was ruined.

Worst of all was the looks I'd received. The pity in everyone's eyes was so insufferable that I barely left my office.

My afternoon consisted of seven meetings, during all of which I'd thought about that night in the abandoned storehouse while officials blabbered on and on about budgets and the closed border and what might happen if we pulled our investments out of the Plexus.

Leid was right. I wasn't ready to be here. I didn't know if I could *ever* be here again.

Yet this was my life, and I couldn't escape it no matter how much I wanted to.

Leid called me on her lunch break and we spoke for a while about my day. I told her I was doing fine, and she knew that I was lying.

We all had dinner together before heading to Moritoria for Tae's pyre. It was the most awkward thing I'd ever sat through. I barely ate anything, as did Roen, and the majority of our time was spent in solemn silence. Ila and Leid kept trying to strike conversation, but it never held. All we did was look at each other, dreading the night to follow. Once my sister was burned, she was officially gone.

After the ceremony, we hung around and watched the smoke disappear into the night sky. A priest conserved Tae's ashes, but I told him to scatter them over the Areva.

Roen was the first to leave, teary-eyed and withdrawn. I watched his silhouette wander away through the field. He had lost his wife and unborn child—*his entire family*—in one night, and I was disgusted with myself for feeling a trace of satisfaction at his suffering. I didn't feel as alone, as fucked up as that sounded.

The rest of us departed with promises of getting together again soon. Leid and I returned to Eroqam without any conversation. When we got to our estate, she made a beeline for our liquor cabinet, and I headed to our bedroom.

She was having a rough time, I knew. Leid had loved my sister as much as me. Even though I pretended to be fine, she knew I wasn't and had to be the strong one.

My wife had to be the strong one. I felt so pathetic.

I turned off the lamp and slid under the covers, curling on my side, feeling the heavy thunder in my chest. I'd gotten hardly any sleep since Tae's death. I wasn't tired, even now. Any attempt at slumber was interrupted by terrifying nightmares, and now I was too afraid to even try.

I laid there in the dark until light cracked against the wall. It faded, and a moment later Leid was beside me. The warmth of her body relaxed me slightly, and she nuzzled her way between my arms. She cupped my face and we stared at each other, nose-to-nose, saying nothing yet everything at the same time.

"I'm sorry," she whispered. "I'm sorry that this is so hard for you. I wish I could fix it, but the only remedy is time."

Time.

That wasn't good enough. I wouldn't let Tae become some distant memory like my mother. The thought of one day forgetting her face made my chest heavy. Leid realized she'd said the wrong thing, but it was too late. I pulled away and sat up, rubbing my throbbing head.

"Qaira, please, you *have* to sleep."

"I can't."

"You aren't doing your sanity any good by staying up for days on end!"

"Don't you think I know that?!" I shouted. *"You really think I* don't *want to sleep? Do you really think I* want *to feel like this?!"*

She looked away, scathed.

"I'm sorry," I mumbled. "I didn't mean to yell."

Before Leid could respond, I was out of bed and grabbing a jacket.

"Where are you going?"

"Out."

"Out where? It's past midnight."

"To clear my head. I need some time to think."

"Qaira—"

"Since when do I need your permission?"

I slammed the door.

She didn't follow me.

***

Leid was right, as always; I needed sleep.

So here I was, parked at a vacant lot behind a grain storage facility, cradling a loaded syringe. Its contents shined effervescent violet in the streetlamps, and the longer I stared, the further my heart sank.

But I could still remember malay's numbness, and I yearned for that feeling more than ever. What I needed now was impalpability. I wanted to feel nothing; think nothing.

Acquiring the syringe wasn't difficult. Ara had several informants across Sanctum who were dealers, one of whom used to be mine. He'd handed over the syringe with a confused look, asking why I'd ever want to take it again.

"You're the only person I know who's made it out clean. Dozens of people give up and die trying to get off the 'lay, but you want another go?"

I'd shoved money into his hand, leaving that question hanging.

I removed my jacket and rolled up my sleeve. My arm was smooth and perfect, free of tracks, and just the thought of that needle marring my skin made my stomach clench.

Don't think. Just do it.

I closed my eyes and pushed the needle into my vein, the sting familiar, yet foreign. My thumb pressed down on the syringe cap, ejecting half of the canister into my bloodstream. I wouldn't take the whole dose, as I'd been clean for ten years and something that heavy might kill me.

I sat there and waited, and waited, *and waited*—but the high never came. Had the dealer sold me crap?

After waiting another several minutes, I unloaded the rest of the syringe in an act of desperation. But halfway through the second dose, the first dose kicked in. It was latent. Malay had evolved since I'd taken it last, and before I realized what was happening, the syringe was empty.

"No," I whispered, tachycardia already setting in. My mind exploded with rapid-fire thoughts, none of them the least bit cohesive. There were starbursts behind my eyes, and I couldn't unclench my legs.

I reached for the door but my hands wouldn't work. This time there was no euphoria, only terror. I had overdosed and they were going to find me in the morning, dead in my craft with an empty syringe cartridge. What would everyone think? What would Leid think?

"No," I said again, trying to uncurl my trembling fists. But the light from my eyes was fading. A tunnel formed in front of me, a mass of swirling darkness getting tighter and tighter by the second. My chest cramped and my eyes rolled into my head, and the last thing I felt was my head hitting the passenger seat.

***

I was *vomiting*.

My eyes shot open as bile and acid were expunged from my throat, leaving a sharp tingle down my spine and a hot, bitter burn in my mouth.

My head was halfway out of the craft, the door wide open, and I'd woken up in the middle of the act. There was already a substantial puddle of puke below.

The pain was so intense that I clamped my lips shut, trying to stave back another wave. My eyes watered and my sinuses felt like they were on fire. I recoiled into the chair and held my face. My stomach heaved. More vomit erupted up my throat but I swallowed it down.

None of this had gone as I'd planned.

I looked at the sky, the darkness receding to cloudy indigo, a tell-tale sign that dawn was fast approaching. I'd lost a lot of time, and no doubt Leid was looking for me. Maybe she'd even called my brother by now and they *both* were looking for me.

I had to get out of here.

My shaking, sweating hand reached for the ignition key, but then I noticed a shadow in my peripherals. My head shot right, and I froze.

Calenus Karim was sitting in the passenger seat, staring out the windshield.

I said nothing. I didn't move.

His eyes slid to me, and he smiled. "You're welcome."

"What the fuck?"

"If not for me you would have been covered in your own spew." His gaze drew downward, and he nodded. "You might want to do something about that."

I followed his stare. The needle was still in my arm. I ripped it out, tossing the syringe out the window.

"I have to say, stalking you has never posed a dull moment."

"What are you doing here?"

"The same could be asked of you."

"What I do is none of your business. Get out of my craft."

"Such hostility; even after I saved your life."

"You didn't save my life. You set me free but left my sister to die."

Calenus looked away, a frown pulling at his lips. "She was already dead."

I didn't respond, holding my head. The nausea had given way to a migraine.

"You know what I'm doing here, Regent, and you know how to make me go away."

I shook my head.

"You might think your life can't get any worse, but it will, and so will everyone else's. Leid has to come back."

"You can stalk me forever, but I'm not driving her away. Actually, you're kind of convenient to have around."

"My convenience is only temporary. This is the last time that I'm placing the offer on the table."

Our eyes met again, and the halcyon of his look was gone. There was desperation and menace behind his gaze, no matter how hard he feigned calm.

"No," I said. "Take your offer and get the fuck out of here."

Leid was the only thing that I had left. I wouldn't let her be taken from me, too.

Calenus sighed and lowered his head, threads of long, black hair hiding his face. "Very well. You've made your bed, Regent."

He opened the door and stepped out of the craft, leaning in through the window. His eyes were glowing. "But make no mistake, we will meet again, and when that happens I will be the last thing you'll ever see."

His threat left me cold, and I threw open the dash to grab my gun. As Calenus walked out of the lot and down the street, I took chase, aiming at his shadow.

"Stop!" I shouted.

He didn't look back.

A second later, he vanished.

I stood there, staring at the place he'd been. A part of me was convinced that this had all been a malay-induced hallucination, but I knew better.

There was movement in the corner of my eye, and I spun, aiming my weapon at the threat. But it was only my reflection in the glass panes of a high-rise.

I didn't even recognize myself. My eyes were blood-shot and crazy, framed by dark circles from stress and sleep deprivation, and my skin shined with a sickly coat of sweat.

You have to get out of here, said Logic. *Before someone sees you pointing a gun at your own reflection.*

I shoved the gun in my belt, turning to leave, but then something caught my eye in the pane. Someone was behind me.

… *Tae.*

She looked how she had in her final moments. Broken, *suffering.* Her eyes screamed for help, and the bloody chain around her neck swayed and jingled with her approach.

I closed my eyes, trying to wish away the image. But she was still there. *Closer.*

Tae wrapped her arms around my shoulders, her bloody stump oozing red across my shirt. Her mangled, torn wings fluttered, spraying blood against the pane. She lifted her chin and her blue, post-partum lips grazed my ear.

I felt it.

I actually *felt* the whisper, warm and soft against the cold, morning air. Tae told me that she loved me, and that she forgave me...

And then she told me how to free us of our torment.

XII
WITHIN REASON

Two minutes from lunch, my aeon chimed.

It was annoying because I was really, *really* hungry and been rushing to sign a few budget approvals so I could take an early lunch.

I answered the call. My secretary informed me that my brother was waiting outside. Ara never scheduled appointments. He didn't have to; we were family.

Ignoring my rumbling stomach, I told her to send him in. Hopefully what he had to say wouldn't take too long.

My brother stepped inside, closing the door behind him. He looked troubled, *nervous*.

"Have you eaten?" I asked.

"Yeah, I ate a late breakfast." He paused, battling a thought. "Qaira, I don't agree with this."

"Don't agree with what?"

"Closing the borders."

It had pained me to hear him say that, but I understood why. Sanctum's economy depended on our partnership with Heaven. Yet the pain came from the idea that he was placing our economy over our honor—a clear demonstration that we were becoming *like* the angels. Ten years ago Ara would have followed me into Maghir's Ocean, and now he was protesting vengeance for our murdered sister.

111

"I see."

"I don't believe that Commander Raith had a hand in Tae's death."

"Then why did Micah Triev say he did?"

"Maybe another war is what he wants. Maybe he's hoping you'll believe Raith is guilty. You could be playing into his hand."

"He meant to kill me, Ara. If I hadn't gotten free, his men would have killed me after Tae. So *why* would he tell me about Lucifer's involvement?"

Ara sighed, sinking to the couch. "I don't know. Even if Lucifer is involved, we can't go to war with them. Not again. We don't have the means."

My eyes lowered to the stack of budget approvals. "I know."

My brother looked surprised. "You do?"

"I closed Sanctum's border to bide some time. It was a political mess, and I wasn't in the right mindset to make any decisions or statements last week. Our quarantine was strictly defensive. I couldn't risk another act of terrorism. From *either* side. Lucifer and I are meeting over telecom this afternoon to smooth out the wrinkles."

Ara reclined in his seat, relieved. "You've changed so much, you know."

"… Have I?"

"And you could have said something sooner. That would have saved me thirty minutes practicing my opinion in front of the mirror."

I laughed, and so did he.

On his way out, I said, "Have your wife call me tonight. I want to speak to her about booking a spot at Yema."

He lingered in the doorway, blinking. "For what?"

"It's a surprise. I'll tell you once I've made further arrangements."

"You know how much I *love* surprises," Ara muttered, shutting the door.

***

The telecom flashed, and with it my heart thumped in my chest.

Lucifer appeared, materializing on screen with a cautious look in his eyes. A scarlet mantle was draped over his right arm—no doubt to cover his hand—and his ice-blonde hair was twisted in a braid that fell across his shoulder, disappearing off-screen. The room beyond was vacant, as was mine. We'd decided to converse in private. I'd sent out all my CAs after they had activated Crylle's feed.

When I said nothing, only stared, he chose to break the ice. "I understand why you're upset."

"Yeah?" I asked, near-whisper.

"What can I do to prove that I wasn't involved with your sister's murder? What would you like to hear me say?"

I reclined in my seat. "Save your groveling. I'm not here to fight."

Lucifer tilted his head.

"Things have been... *difficult,*" I began. "I segregated Sanctum for some time to think."

"And what's your conclusion?"

"A peace ceremony."

Lucifer stared at me like I'd just shat a rainbow. "A...peace ceremony."

"A lot of things have been brought to light. Neither of our cities will prevail under cold war. In only a week our economy has dropped a quarter. Parliament's in disarray."

"And what about you?"

I paused. "Come again?"

"You've given me reasons for continued peace based on the desires of your city and its subjects. But what about you?"

My stare hardened. "What about me?"

"I want you to believe that I didn't order your sister's death. I can't keep an alliance with a city whose ruler doesn't trust me."

Raith looked so sincere, and that really bugged me. "I believe you."

He hesitated, searching my face for the tiniest fracture. He wouldn't find any, because I had practiced apathy my entire life. "Tell me more about the peace ceremony."

"I want to hold an event at Yema Theater; Archaeans and Nehelians united under one roof to celebrate our alliance."

"When?"

"Not sure yet. I have to talk to Yema's curator."

"What would the ceremony entail?"

"Speeches, music, performances—whatever you see fit. We'll invite the media. That should cool down the talk of war."

"How many people can Yema hold?"

"Twenty thousand, full house. Ten thousand angels and Nehelians."

Lucifer grew silent, thinking.

"Are you onboard?" I pressed.

"If I agree, will you send your scientists back to the Plexus? Yahweh is very upset about that."

"I plan to reopen the borders after I make a statement to the press. The Plexus will be replenished soon after."

Raith smiled. "Then count me in."

"I'll call you again when I know more details. In the meantime, think of ways we might entertain our audience."

"I look forward to our talk, Qaira."

I severed the call and the feed blipped to static. I watched, the warmth in my expression dwindling. Then, I left the communications room and headed back to Parliament. The first thing I did when I returned to my office was schedule a meeting with Director Kada Ysam.

O
AMISS

Yahweh Telei—;

THE YOUNG BOY OPENED HIS MOUTH AND I pressed the wooden spatula against his tongue. Usually I had to squint in order to see the state of someone's throat, but not his.

"Erynotitis," I said, and the boy coughed. His mother rubbed his shoulder, easing him. "I'll write you a script for antibiotics."

Seldom did I practice medicine anymore, but I tried to help out at Adonai Hospital once a month. As CEO of the Plexus, my physician coat had been replaced by a business suit, patients replaced by *patents*—so it was good to get out of my office and treat sick people every now and again.

As the woman and her son shuffled out of the examination room, script in hand, a nurse poked her head inside.

"Dr. Telei, there's a call for you."

"Thank you," I said, following her to the reception desk. I touched the rune on the Aeon, gazing ahead.

This is Dr. Telei.

Yahweh, it's Namah.

... Dr. Ipsin, you're two floors down.

That's two floors too far. I've got a line of patients and can't leave the unit.

What do you need?

There's been a spike in pharyngitis and emphysema-type cases over the past two weeks. Have you noticed?

Can't say that I have.

The patients aren't responding to antibiotics and blood tests show nothing but an extraordinary count of leukocytes.

Viral?

If it's viral, it's taking a very long time to clear up. I've just scheduled a chest irridigram for a patient who's suffered emphysema for almost three weeks. I've got a few other cases here under review and wanted you to take a look at them.

Can you send them to my office at the Plexus? I'll be there later this afternoon.

Sure. When can I expect to hear back from you?

Tomorrow afternoon at the latest.

Until then.

***

On my way back to Moritoria, I made a detour to *Theosyne*, Heaven's governing house, to check on the status of Sanctum's segregation. We were hit hard by Qaira's decision to pull our Nehelian employees from the Plexus. Production and research had been cut in half, and the Axium clinical trial was collecting dust.

Lucifer had planned to speak to Qaira this afternoon, and I wanted to know what was happening. I found my father emerging from our panels room, evidently having just talked to the Regent. There was a look on his face that spoke of trouble. I was almost too afraid to ask.

"A peace ceremony," said Lucifer, just as I opened my mouth.

"… Sorry?"

"He wants us to hold a peace ceremony in Sanctum. Ten thousand angels are invited."

Qaira was trying to mend our alliance. That should have been good news; why did Lucifer look so jaded?

And then I thought about it.

That didn't sound like Qaira Eltruan. He was never *that* diplomatic, even in peace. Perhaps Leid had influenced his idea, but...

No, something was amiss.

"He's reopening the borders tomorrow," my father continued, walking through the hall. I followed. "The Plexus will have its scientists back after he makes a statement to the press."

"Just like that?"

"Exactly," he muttered.

"What do you think?"

"I don't know yet. For now I'm onboard with the idea, but instinct warns mindfulness. He said he believed that I wasn't involved in Tae's death, but his face said otherwise."

"Do you think it's a trap?"

Lucifer unlocked his office, letting me in first. Once we were out of ear's reach, he said, "That's the confusing bit. He wants to hold the peace ceremony at Yema Theater, and ten thousand of his own people will be in the audience, too."

"Why don't you ask for it to be held elsewhere? Somewhere closer to home?"

"I don't think he'd come to Heaven, scheming or not."

"True, but what about Moritoria?"

Lucifer sat at his desk, stroking his chin. "Perhaps."

"Whatever you do, be careful. Qaira isn't stupid."

"I never said he was. Brash, yes. Derogatory, *absolutely*. But never stupid."

I lowered my eyes, recalling the last conversation that I'd had with the Regent. There was a piece of it I had neglected to tell Lucifer, but with the scent of danger in the air, it was best that I did. "He knows."

"Knows what?"

"About Leid."

Lucifer hesitated, staring. His face grew darker as the seconds passed. "You told him?"

"No. Like I said, he isn't stupid. He was able to correlate our discussion in my office with Calenus' appearance. He thinks—*knows*—we've been spying on him."

A little while after we'd settled into The Atrium, only a few weeks after Leid and Qaira were wed, Calenus made a secret visit to the Ark and told us to notify the Court of Enigmus if Leid ever presented any strange *symptoms*.

He hadn't specified what those symptoms were, or why we needed to contact him. When Lucifer inquired about what we should be looking for, Calenus only said, "You'll know, trust me."

And he'd been right. The first thing I'd done after Qaira asked about Leid's black eyes was call Lucifer, who in turn contacted the Court of Enigmus. What I hadn't expected was Calenus' immediate response. So much for subtlety. He'd practically thrown me under the craft.

"He made no mention of that?" I asked.

"No."

Another red flag.

"Any news on Micah Triev?"

Lucifer only shook his head; our conversation was wearing on him. He looked tired. Stress was his only friend as of late.

We needed to find Micah if we ever hoped to reconcile with Sanctum. The longer he was missing, the guiltier we looked. Lucifer knew that, so I didn't bother saying anything. How Triev had been able to shake authorities for so long was a mystery.

"Are you hungry?" I offered. "I haven't eaten lunch yet."

"Not really," he said. "But you're free to stay and order service."

"No, I'll eat when I get back to my office. It just looks like you need to unwind a bit."

He laughed mirthlessly. "Thanks for the advice. That coming from you, I'm in big trouble."

***

Coffee, *check*.

Early dinner, *check.*

Strings music playing listlessly in the background, *check.*

Time to look at those case files.

Namah had made them accessible via the Plexus' private database. I typed in the administration code and downloaded the files, waiting for them to load onscreen. While I waited I took a bite of my meat pastry. It was dry, but I was hungry enough to ignore that flaw.

Sonaius, XXII – Year 451360:

Patient Name: Samael Soran

Age: 3020   Weight: 85 lu   Height: 6'1"   G: M

The patient was admitted at 11:30 PM with chief complaints of chest tightness, apnea, and chest pain. Initial examination showed wheezing and pleurisy. An upper respiratory biopsy was carried out after physical examination. Mast cells and lymphocyte proliferation found within interpleural tissues. Cause of inflammation is unknown. Blood tests showed negative for pathogenic substrates or toxins.

I scrolled through the results, frowning thoughtfully.

There were ten more identical cases, enough to pique my concern. It must have killed Namah to ask for my help. He never failed to show how seasoned he was in our field.

After reading the cases, I reached for the Aeon. It was after clinic hours so I called his apartment line.

Hello?

It's me.

Earlier than I expected.

Yes, you've caught my interest. What time did you schedule that chest irridigram?

Tomorrow afternoon.

Send the results to me, if you can.

I certainly will.

Removing my finger from the rune, I took another bite of dinner, re-reading the case files. Perhaps the Plexus had another project lined up.

My eyes rose to the muted televised screen on the wall across from my desk. A Sanctum PB headline scrolled along the right panel, titled:

REGENT DENOUNCES COLD WAR—BORDERS REOPENED TOMORROW

I selected the headline and Qaira's statement played. I turned up the volume, listening to his speech. He spoke of mending wounds and getting past the tragedy that befell Sanctum. Promises of lasting peace and productivity filled the ears of his audience, but Qaira delivered them with dead eyes. He'd worn the same look when I first met him.

It was just as I thought.

This wasn't over.

XIII
PERTINENCE OF RESPECT

MY CITY LOOKED SO FOREIGN.

Coua replaced by glass pane, aeroways decorated by lights and digital advertisement boards, crafts sleeker and flashier, smaller yet more efficient. The only constant was the bleak, gray sky.

Sanctum had become a derivative of Crylle. Parliament and its people worshipped angel technology, begging for more and more of it. *Convenience* was a currency valued over usos, reducing people to frothy-mouthed, crazy-eyed goons. If we kept on like this, there would be a price. I didn't know what that price was, but I knew there was one. There was always a price.

Winter was in full-effect, covering Sanctum in snow, sleet or rain day-round. Sometimes all three at once. Right now it was raining and I leant against the sill of my office window, watching beads of partially frozen water tap the glass, sipping a cup of hot coffee.

I'd slept for four hours last night, a new record since my sister's death. Leid woke up early and we had breakfast at a shop near Parliament.

It was getting easier to feign normalcy. Smiles were fluid, albeit with effort, and small talk was manageable. The ever-present concern on my wife's face had diminished as of this morning. The statement I'd made yesterday had pleased her, and it broke my heart knowing that now I had to please her as well. I had to please everyone—all part of the job—but she and I had always been unprejudiced. *Candid.* It was almost like Leid had died, too.

The Aeon chimed and my secretary announced that Dr. Ysam was here. After instructing her to bring him in, I resumed my spot at the window, finishing my coffee.

Dr. Kada Ysam was the Director of Eroqam Research Science and had headed the team responsible for upgrading our military crafts during the war. Yahweh and Lucifer had pressed to recruit him to the Plexus, but Ysam declined.

He didn't like angels.

As diplomatic as he seemed, he was never onboard with the whites. Kada had led several government protests against angel migration when our alliance was formed. They all were peaceful protests, given his rank and placement, but now his hate was something I needed. He had lost his son fifty years ago, after the angels' first strike on Sanctum. Dr. Ysam would be sympathetic to my cause.

"Qaira," Kada greeted, closing the door behind him. "This is a surprise."

"It's been too long, Doctor."

"Yes," he said, taking a seat. The look he gave me said much more than that, something like, *'Too long that you've been friendly with the whites.'*

He was close to my father's age—when my father had been alive, that is. Tall and dark, always dressed in black, with raven hair cropped short to his head, graying at the temples.

"What's this about?" asked Kada when I'd failed to say anything else, drawn again to the window.

"It's been too long," I repeated, and this time he caught my drift.

"I'm sorry about Tae," he said, quietly. "Believe me when I say I know exactly what you're going through."

"You saw my statement?"

"I did. Can't say I approve."

"Good."

Kada fell silent, startled. I left the window and sat behind my desk.

"I'm planning a peace ceremony at Yema Theater, two weeks from today. I've invited Commander Raith and ten thousand angels to attend. There will be speeches, art performances—a mosaic of culture under one roof."

Kada said nothing, his confusion growing ten-fold.

"Our Research Science department has angel devices, does it not?"

"Define *devices*."

"Explosives."

The confusion in Kada eyes waned. "Yes, it does. What kind of explosives?"

"Demolition."

"… You want to bring down Yema Theater with the angels inside."

I didn't respond, but my expression verified that claim.

"And how do you expect to get away with it? If you kill that many angels on Sanctum ground, you'll be convicted of a war crime."

"They won't look to me. The evidence will point toward another act of angel terrorism."

"Why would the angels want to kill their own people?"

"Not only their people."

Kada hesitated, darkening. "How many?"

"Many."

Ten thousand.

Ten thousand Nehelians were to be sacrificed, but the means justified the end. Our city would revolt against the angels and no one would push for peace any longer. They would want blood. They would want war.

And this time we'd win, because Lucifer Raith would be buried under the ruins of Yema Theater, his Heaven left leaderless. *Powerless*, like pouring water on a hive and watching all the little insects scramble out—desperate, terrified.

"Qaira, that's… a heavy burden to carry."

"I've carried heavier, sadly," I murmured, looking away. When Kada said nothing, I continued, "The angels must be erased. I've discovered that Commander Raith was responsible for my sister's death. The Nehelian decree is honor, no matter the price. And we've lost that honor; we've lost our identity because the whites have bleached our pond with fancy gadgets and apathy."

Kada lowered his gaze, nodding. "You're the Regent. Even if I don't morally agree with your plan, I'm at your disposal."

"You don't agree with my plan?"

"I agree that the angels need gone, but I don't agree with the method."

"I know this will sound unfeeling, but the Nehelians to attend our peace ceremony are angel-lovers. Sympathizers. They would only get in the way of any future conflict."

Surprisingly, Kada saw reason in that. The indecision on him faded. "You have my fealty."

I bowed my head, grateful. "Gather employees whom you know you can trust. I'll call you in a few days and schedule another meeting at Eroqam."

As Kada moved to leave, the Aeon chimed again.

Yes?

Sir, Roen Artuega is demanding to speak to you.

I eyed the clock; only ten minutes until a sit-down with the Education Department. *I don't have time for walk-ins.*

He's not taking no for an answer. He's quite belligerent, sir. I think he's been drinking.

Fuck me.

Reschedule for noon, then. I can't see him right now.

But the call was already cut. Kada had left, thankfully, and my eyes rose to the sound of incoming voices. Angry voices.

The door exploded open, revealing my secretary and brother-in-law engaged in a screaming match. I stood, startled.

"The Regent is not seeing anyone!" my secretary exclaimed, looking to me for help.

"You!" Roen shouted, pointing in my general direction. She was right, he was loaded. "I have words to say to you, you coward! *You coward!"*

"Leave us," I said to my secretary. "Close the door."

Once alone, Roen composed himself. Or tried to.

He was a wreck. Red-faced with eyes so bloodshot that they almost matched his tie, which looked like it had been tied around his collar by a child. Clearly he had been drinking for a long while, and it was only eight in the morning.

Roen moved to sit, but lurched and vomited all over my floor instead.

"Oh, Maghir!" I exclaimed, unable to believe my eyes. *"What the fuck—!?"*

"How could you?" he slurred, heavy-breathed. "Those monsters butchered your sister and all's forgiven? You told our people that the alliance is *everlasting?"*

My anger waned. I sank back into my seat, saying nothing.

"They raped and tortured my wife—*your sister*—and you're not going to do anything about it?"

"Sit down."

"I believed in you. I always thought you were different than the other bureaucratic sifts, but I was wrong. You'd let the angels get away with this."

"Sit down," I repeated, this time through my teeth.

"You're a coward," Roen hissed, deaf to my demand. Evidently he had no desire to listen to reason and had only come here to say his piece.

He was wrong. I *was* different than the other suits, but my plans were well beyond his trust. Technically Roen wasn't even family anymore. All the better; I never liked him much anyway.

There was a pen resting beside a stack of folders to which I had yet to attend. I grabbed it. My estranged brother-in-law was too far gone to acknowledge the warning in my eyes.

"They've taken everything from me," he went on, spitting his disgust. "And now they're off scot-free while I'm left to rot."

The pen shook in my hand.

"And her own brother, the only man with any power in this Maghir-forsaken city, sits behind his desk and assures us of peace. You didn't love her at all, did you? *You heartless fuck, you didn't love her at all!*"

I lunged over the desk and grabbed Roen by his poor excuse for a tie. He fell forward and I jammed my pen through his eye. A scream channeled from his mouth as watery blood streamed down his face, but I pulled his tie tighter, cutting off his wind. Even tighter and he was inches from my face.

"Tae will be avenged," I whispered. "But you will never see that day."

I dislodged the pen and threw him through the window. Glass exploded as he fell, and I surveyed his hundred story plummet. Roen's body hit the port like a water balloon; all that was left was a giant red stain across white cement.

I pocketed the pen as the door opened. My secretary stared at me with wide, frightened eyes, having heard the commotion from her desk. I mimicked her look.

"Regent, what happened?!"

I held my head, grief-stricken. "He… h-he jumped."

XIV
GOOD INTENTIONS

"AND THEN HE JUMPED?" Ara asked, wide-eyed.

I nodded solemnly, trying not to meet his gaze.

We were sitting in his home at Upper Sanctum Gardens, a three-estate terrace that overlooked the Agora. It was the early afternoon, and I'd been here since the authorities had closed my office for investigation. Ara took the rest of the day off as his men scraped Roen from the port and staved off Sanctum PB. Rumors were already spreading and the media had identified the body, despite our best efforts to conceal any information.

Roen's suicide rekindled my sister's death, which swept like wildfire across every station throughout the city. I was already thinking of the statement that I'd have to make. Sometimes I just wanted to curl up under a rock and disappear forever.

We ate take-away lunch while I told him what had happened. Well, I told him what I wanted him to think happened. I left out the part about stabbing Roen in the face and tossing him out the window. The rest was true, though.

My brother shook his head, looking over the balcony. "That's fucked up. Couldn't swallow the grief, I guess. Ila's invited him over for dinner a thousand times since…" He paused, shaking his head again. Ara never spoke of Tae's murder. "And he always

127

brushed us off. According to my men, Ro was removed from chair three days ago. Director said he was hostile and withdrawn, and he couldn't sympathize any longer. My guess is he's been binge drinking and stewing ever since."

"He didn't like my statement."

"Clearly."

I took a sip of wine, glancing over the gray wash of Sanctum's city-scape. To be fair, I hadn't liked my statement either. But Roen's hostility had come as a surprise, as I'd assumed continued peace with the angels was what everyone wanted. How many others wished for vengeance in my sister's name? Not Ara, painfully enough, yet knowing at least *someone* felt the same way as me made the ice melt a bit.

It was a shame Roen had been so weak and useless. I'd regretted killing him after the anger faded, but it didn't ruin me. Little could these days.

"Have you talked to Leid yet?"

I shook my head. "She probably hasn't even seen the news; she's instructing classes all day."

"Shouldn't you call her?"

"And ruin her day as well?"

"Yeah, good point."

We sipped our drinks in silence. The wind blew our lunch wrappers across the table, and Ara caught them before they were swept off the balcony. "It's going to rain again," he said, looking at the sky. "This winter's been mild."

I didn't reply, huddling into my coat. Winter was mild, but I was still freezing my ass off. "I should go. I need to get a statement ready."

"I don't envy you," he said. "Every time something happens, you have to tell the world about it."

I smiled, sadly. "I don't know how Dad did it."

"I don't know how *you* do it."

I didn't. Ninety percent of what I said in front of the cameras was a lie. Spin was advantageous, if you knew how to play it. I stood from the table and patted Ara on the shoulder. "I'll call you later."

***

Leid was remarkably stoic after I'd told her the news at dinner. At least I thought so, until she slipped away and played her cello in the music room for the rest of the night. Her songs were sadder than usual.

I sat there listening as I crafted my statement, the cadence influencing my script. It took much longer than usual because I kept accidentally writing truth in what needed to be a total lie.

Well past bedtime, Leid hadn't returned. The music kept flowing and it was driving me insane. I didn't like it when my wife was upset, and I couldn't go to sleep knowing that she was. I headed to the music room to fetch her, but right before I entered, her cello stopped.

She gazed at me from the doorway, somber, listless. Sweat dripped from her temples and her pale ivory blouse was soaked. I stared at her, concerned.

Before I could say anything she set her cello aside and rose from the stool, walking slowly toward me. Leid placed a hand against my chest and lifted her chin, looking me in the eyes. The lights overhead cast a glimmer in her gaze. I couldn't read her thoughts.

"I want to see your wings," she said.

"Not here."

"Then somewhere else."

She led me to the port, all the while I wondered what was going through her mind. Leid was spontaneous—such a random request wasn't unusual, but somehow her spontaneity still managed to catch me off guard every time.

The port was vacant, and had been ever since Eroqam dissolved its military wing. Once there, Leid stepped back and waited.

"I'm not wearing flight clothes," I protested, suddenly feeling vulnerable. The fact that she could still make me feel like this was stunning.

"Then take them off."

I arched my brows. "What?"

"Take off your clothes."

"… What are you doing?"

"I want to see your wings."

I sighed, removing my shirt. Once Leid got an idea into her head, there was no stopping her. I'd learned that the hard way.

My shoulders flexed and my wings slid from their *membranes*—tiny slits beside each shoulder blade. They quivered, shaking off viscera, and then spread to full breadth. Each wing was seven feet long, which was why I couldn't release them in most areas of our estate. In fact I couldn't remember the last time I'd released them at all. Progress had diminished our need of them, what with crafts and close-quarter living. Once upon a time we were savages with sticks and rocks, hunting game by spears and wings.

Leid re-approached, looking on at my wings in awe. She reached up and ran her fingers across the edges, making me shudder. "It's been so long since I've seen them," she murmured. "They're beautiful. *Godly.*"

I said nothing, watching her. She had always been tiny, but seemed even tinier now with my wings fully spread. She looked at me with child-like wonder, and for a second I pictured her eyes black. But they never turned black. They stayed beautifully violet.

And then everything hit me at once; Calenus' threat, Tae's murder, Roen's *suicide*, my plans for the peace ceremony…

I wanted none of this. I would have given anything, *anything*, to return to the days where all we had done was worked, played music, drank wine, and then ravaged each other 'til the early morning.

But those days were gone. Such a harrowing truth.

Leid furrowed her brows, reaching for my face. "Qaira?"

I looked away, choking back tears. She thought I was crying for Roen, and I let her. She pressed her cheek to my chest, tracing the ink across my stomach. The soft, methodical feel of her finger settled my tumult. My breathing slowed, steadied.

She was still everything to me. In all this chaos, I had forgotten how much I loved her.

I couldn't lose her. *Not her.*

My wings folded around Leid, and she kept me warm in the cold, quiet darkness.

XV
EQUAL FIRE

My sister was stalking me.

Tae appeared within every window and mirror, looking more grotesque and feral each time. Yet her charge was always the same: vengeance.

It'd grown so terrifying that I avoided my reflection at all costs. I had no idea what I even looked like today, because I'd gotten ready for work without a mirror. My only hope was that as soon as Raith was dead, Tae could finally rest in peace.

I had also entertained the thought that I was going crazy, but, really, that was irrelevant; even *if* that were true, my temporary slip of sanity should be cured if I appeased that sick part of my mind. Either way, Lucifer had to die.

Kada and his team of engineers were working on setting the explosives at Yema Theater. I had cleared a spot there all morning, informing Ila that we were closing it for refurnishing. That was happening too, but later today.

Meanwhile I spent the morning in my office, dealing with meetings and other routine projects. Business as usual.

I'd noticed Leid had set tulan steaks out to thaw before she left for work, and I checked my calendar as soon as I got in, making sure I wasn't forgetting a special occasion. Leid never made anything other than leriza, except on special occasions like my birthday, our anniversary, etc. But as far as I could tell, this wasn't a special occasion. The mystery surrounding those steaks haunted me all morning.

Two representatives from the Board of Commerce just left my office, and I was preparing to crack down on a stack of budget proposals and business projections that had grown taller by the hour. As I reached for my pen, my Aeon chimed.

I stared at it, fantasizing about smashing it to little pieces. Instead I answered the call.

Yes?

Regent, Commander Raith is on wave four, he says it's urgent.

Fantastic.

Alright, connect me through.

My mind grew fuzzy for a second. I hated transferring lines on Aeon. I'd had a constant migraine the first week it was installed.

Good morning, Regent. I hope I'm not interrupting anything?

...Nope.

Swell, because I'm en route to Sanctum as we speak.

I almost exploded out of my chair. *What?*

Your peace ceremony has gotten me excited. I'd like to see the venue, if you don't mind.

Oh, no.

No, no, *no.*

It's closed for refurnishing this morning, I said, floundering. *Can we reschedule?*

Just the same, I wouldn't mind seeing the progress. I'm already in Moritoria so it would be a shame to have to turn around.

This wasn't about him wanting to see Yema out of excitement. He was coming here to inspect it. This was an ambush.

My heart fluttered as I glanced at my watch. Twenty minutes. I had twenty minutes to warn Kada and his team to get those explosives out of there. That wouldn't be enough time.

You're impeding on my lunch, so why don't we eat somewhere first?

134

Lucifer hesitated. *Sure. Where do you have in mind?*

We'll talk about that when you get here. You should have warned me you were coming. It's unceremonious to make me drop everything. That's what my schedule is for.

Again, I'm sorry.

He offered no explanation for the ambush, which only steeled my suspicion.

I'll make an exception just this once. See you soon.

***

Feigning innocence was a lot easier over telecomm or Aeon than in person.

I watched Lucifer mull over menu selections with a stony gaze. It was like eating out with Leid all over again.

Surprisingly we had only gotten a few looks at Koraez. None of the customers saw us, because surely the sight of the angel commander and their Nehelian Regent would bring Sanctum PB here in a heartbeat. Instead we were led in through the back door, having warned the restaurant prior to our arrival, and were seated in a closed off area usually reserved for special engagements.

Even so, I figured one of the staff would leak the information to PB eventually. I gave it an hour. It would be good publicity nonetheless, considering it looked like Lucifer and I were friendly again.

Commander Raith was dressed in all black, which was rare. It made him seem even paler, his hair even whiter. The dim lights muted his eyes, erasing his irises. He looked like a statue carved from ivory.

When he finally decided, the server took our menus and we reclined, watching each other. Neither of us knew what to say. In the ten years of our alliance, never once did we have lunch together.

"I heard about Tae's husband," he said. "A tragedy. I'm sorry."

I nodded. "Have you thought about any Archaean events for the peace ceremony?"

Raith hesitated, no doubt wondering why I'd tried to change the subject. "Not yet, no. That's part of why I'm here. I want to see what we're working with before I make any plans."

A better excuse, but still weak.

I glanced at my watch again. After I'd gotten off Aeon with Lucifer, I'd called Yema Theater and warned Kada to take the explosives and vacate the premises. I would have to make another excuse to close Yema at a later time to finish 'setting up'. *Frustrating,* but better that than Lucifer finding out. Hopefully Kada had enough sense to call me once they were gone.

"Yahweh was very happy to hear the news. He's insisted on coming to the peace ceremony, too."

That bit of information almost cracked my façade.

Lucifer paused, studying my face.

"Good," I said, evenly. "He always enjoyed boring, diplomatic crap."

He smiled, stirring coffee. "I take it you're not anticipating the ceremony?"

"I never anticipate public speaking events."

"You chose the wrong line of work, then."

"I didn't choose it."

"Ah, yes. I keep forgetting Sanctum is a monarchy."

"Not really."

"No?"

"The chairs of each division are elected by the people, along with the officials that oversee each district. The only thing they can't vote on is Eltruan rule."

"Half monarchy, half democracy." Lucifer rubbed his chin. "Strange."

I shrugged. "Thousands of years ago, an influential priest decided that our family was chosen by Maghir to lead our people. Not much has changed since."

The server brought our food. When he left, Lucifer said, "Aren't you devout?"

"Faith is a catalyst of power. I already have power."

"Mm," he said, glancing away. "Do you want it?"

"… Want what?"

"Power."

I said nothing, confused.

"Would you have taken the throne, given a choice?"

I opened my mouth to reply, but then paused, thinking about that. The involuntary response was *yes*, though truthfully I wasn't sure. Nearly every ill thing that had ever happened to me was directly related to who I was. *My title.*

I decided to leave that question up in the air. "Is the food to your liking?"

Lucifer studied his plate, chewing. "Your food has a lot of flavor."

"You say that like it's a bad thing."

"It is when my lips are still burning an hour after my meal."

I smirked. "Can't take the heat?"

"I'll live."

My Aeon chimed. Kada had sent me a cryptic message stating that Yema was clear.

Lucifer tilted his head. "Is everything alright?"

"Yeah," I mumbled. "Just my secretary."

"She has your private wave?"

"Of course. Doesn't yours?"

"No one is permitted to call me after working hours. I may stay at work late more than a few times per week, but once I leave for the day, that's it."

I blinked. "What if there's an emergency?"

"Define emergency."

"What if someone needs to reschedule a meeting?"

"Then they can reschedule it during business hours."

"I'd prefer leaving on time and having my secretary call me than staying late."

Lucifer smiled. "And I prefer leaving work and not thinking about it at all."

"… How can you not think about your job at all when you're the *Commander?*"

"The angels practice work-life balance. Well, except for Yahweh. But he loves his job, so he doesn't really count. Likewise, my title doesn't define me. Letting your job—especially one like ours—consume your life leaves you open for attack."

"Attack?"

"Stress, anxiety, placing your loved ones second; things like that."

All I did was stare at him like he was talking nonsense.

Lucifer shrugged. "Agree to disagree, as always."

"You ready to see Yema?" I asked, looking at my watch. "I suspect the press will be here any moment and I've got a two o'clock with Division of Health."

He nodded, wiping his mouth with a napkin. For some reason how he'd done that irritated me. Everything about the angels was so… proper. *Genteel*, to the point that it seemed like a gross exaggeration. Moreover, prestige was always heavy in Raith's gaze. He thought he was better than me.

The whites still saw us as savages, but now we were savages with shiny toys.

And as cordial as he was, I couldn't forget that Lucifer was here because he didn't trust me.

We vacated the restaurant, and Lucifer hugged his arms. This morning was colder than usual; the kind that turned your breath to steam. He'd worn a thick, tulan-fur jacket, but it didn't look like it was helping him much. My jacket was much thinner and I wasn't even shivering.

Having angel guests always gave us a good laugh. Even in summer they'd come dressed for an arctic expedition. *They need thicker skin*, my brother had said.

"I don't know how you can endure this cold," Lucifer muttered once we were in my craft.

"And I don't know how you can endure that heat."

He frowned, sipping take-away hot *leio* cider. "Agree to disagree, again."

O

THE PENDULUM STARTS TO SWING

Leid Koseling—;

TODAY MARKED THE TENTH YEAR ANNIVERSARY that Qaira had set me free.

He never remembered, promising each time to mark it on his calendar, but each time he forgot. That was okay, though, because I could never forget.

And every anniversary I surprised him with lunch, showing up unannounced, and he'd get that guilty look on his face once I told him why I was there. To me, this anniversary was more important than our wedding, or birthdays. I didn't even celebrate birthdays, as my age had been lost between time and space.

But ten years ago today, my life had been made anew. That was *like* a birthday, at least.

I released my students twenty minutes early and set out for Parliament, hoping to catch Qaira before lunch. My heart sank at the sight of his closed office door, the shades drawn, and the lights off. He was already gone.

But not all was lost.

His secretary, Dela, was speaking to someone on Aeon. I approached her desk, waiting for her to finish. At the sight of me she severed the call and smiled.

"Leid, good afternoon. I haven't seen you in so long!"

"Good afternoon to you," I said, nodding. "Has Qaira left for lunch?"

"No, he's with Commander Raith."

I blinked. This was the first I'd heard about Lucifer meeting with Qaira. Usually he grumbled about it for days prior. "Commander Raith is in Sanctum?"

"It's the funniest thing," she said, idly twirling a long, black curl. "He showed up unannounced and I overheard them talking about Yema Theater on their way out. Perhaps they're there?"

"I'll try there, then. Thank you, Dela."

I returned to the port, pulling up my hood as the cold winter air bit at my cheeks. The guards at the gate nodded and held open the door, while I murmured thanks in passing. Around here, everyone knew who I was. Privacy was virtually impossible when you were married to the world's most important man.

Aeroway traffic at midday was like morning rush hour. What should have been a ten minute drive took twenty. By the time I pulled into Yema's vacant lot, my lunch break was nearly spent. I wouldn't be able to eat with Qaira, but I could still give him his gift.

It was a fancy watch that had caught his eye at the Agora several weeks ago. He'd muttered something about the price—he never liked spending money, ironically enough—and walked out of the shop. But I knew he'd wanted it.

Qaira's craft wasn't here, either.

Someone else's was, though.

I hopped out of my craft and was about to head toward Yema, but a group of men hurried out, carrying boxes of wires and metal cylinders. I froze, confused.

Among them was Kada Ysam, Director of Science Research. I felt my brows furrow as I tried to understand what he was doing here. Ila told me that they were refurnishing the theater for the upcoming peace ceremony, but...

As multifaceted as Kada was, a furnisher he was not.

I hid behind my craft, watching them load boxes into their own. They returned for more boxes, and I squinted, trying to see inside them. Wires, metal cylinders, keypads—;

My breath caught.

Lucifer had shown up to Sanctum unannounced, and suddenly engineers were hurrying out of Yema with boxes full of dubious content. ... Could it be?

No.

No, it can't.

Qaira was better.

He was feeling better; he'd even said so.

But then I remembered the pain in his eyes that night at Eroqam's port. I'd thought it was because of Roen, yet another tally of Tae's tragedy, but it might have been something *deeper*. Guilt.

I pulled out of the lot before they saw me, flying to Parliament. The return trip felt supersonic. All I could think about was what I'd seen—I didn't know for certain, but I had an idea, and that idea alone filled my heart with razorblades.

Dela hadn't moved since I left. I placed the wrapped gift box on the desk, and she looked up from her computer. "He wasn't there?" she asked.

"No, so I'm going to leave this here. Could you give it to him when he returns?"

"Sure. I'm so sorry, darling. I didn't mean to send you on a scavenger hunt."

I smiled, but it was difficult. "No harm."

Much harm.

My smile ran cold as I turned and headed to the port. Back in my office, I sat at my desk and stared at the Aeon, battling my conscience. Class should have started ten minutes ago, but I couldn't will myself to move.

Should I pretend I hadn't seen it? But what would be the consequence of that? Even if my assumption of what was in those boxes was wrong, could I really risk it? Who could I tell, even?

And then I knew.

I reached for a rune, dialing Ara's office.

XVI
SAFE

YEMA WAS CLEARED FOR VIEWING.

Raith was pleased with the venue, especially its size, and talks of performances ensued. I had no idea what he'd expected to find by ambushing me in the middle of the day, but thankfully his trust was reinstated.

On our way back, Lucifer made me stop at another refreshments stand for more hot leio cider. He'd finally found something here that he could stomach. Rumors of his visit spread far enough that a group of reporters were skirting Sanctum, looking for us. They found as at that shop, and we were bombarded with cameras and questions about the peace ceremony and all that it entailed. I told them I wasn't answering questions at the moment, and a statement would be made later this week.

The reporters backed off, forced to accept my answer. They knew what happened to people who made me angry. Points for my ability—I never needed guards.

Back at Parliament, my secretary waved me over to her desk, producing a giftbox that she'd concealed inside a drawer. "Your wife was by," she said. "Asked me to give this to you."

I took it, puzzled, and then returned to my office. The box held a watch I'd seen at the Agora a few weeks ago, and I smirked at her perceptiveness. The watch was wrapped in a piece of paper, which read, *'Happy Anniversary. You've forgotten again, but I never will.'*

"Damnit," I mumbled, remembering the date. Today was the day that the Court of Enigmus had stormed Eroqam, demanding Leid. I'd forgotten *every* year.

At least the mystery of the tulan steaks was cracked.

I called my secretary, requesting that she order a bouquet. I had the rest of the afternoon to think of how else to match her gift. Flowers alone wouldn't cut it.

In the meantime, I marked our anniversary in my digital calendar, making sure I would never forget again.

O
TURBULENCE

Yahweh Telei—;

I MET WITH LUCIFER ON THEOSYNE PORT, eyebrows arched, awaiting his verdict. When he said nothing, only frowned, I pressed. "Well?"

"I'm still not sure," he said, hushed. We walked through the court garden, passing statues and rows of flowers framed by white-picket. Our culture still called for elegance, albeit with crafts roaring overhead. "And I have a terrible stomach ache."

"You ate the food, didn't you? I told you not to eat the food."

"Qaira offered, and it would have been rude to decline."

"So what now, you ambush him again? The ceremony is in a week."

"No, I think I've made it evident enough that I don't trust him. This is delicate all around, and any further harassment might turn his offer sour. Even though I'm not completely sure the peace ceremony isn't a rouse, there's no choice now but to proceed."

I hid my delight, nodding. Although I suspected Qaira wasn't over his suspicion of us, had Lucifer found anything potentially dangerous at Yema, he would have pulled the plug immediately. Perhaps I'd been wrong, and being wrong never felt so wonderful.

My Aeon chimed, vibrating against my hip. I pulled it from my pocket and inspected the frequency. Namah, *again*.

"I'm needed back at the Plexus," I said, cancelling the call. I'd speak to Dr. Ipsin in Moritoria.

"I'll see you at home, then. I've got a busy afternoon ahead of me, what with chasing down our local entertainment to see who wants to volunteer in Sanctum."

I snorted. "Have fun with that. When will you make the announcement?"

"As soon as Qaira makes his."

We said our goodbyes and parted ways.

***

The inflammation is strange, I said, studying pictures of the chest irridigram that Nahamh had sent over. *The blood tests show nothing?*

Nothing, confirmed Namah. *No pathogens, and every viral test I've performed turned up nothing either. We just received four more patients with early symptoms today. I don't want to alarm you, but it's starting to look like an epidemic.*

I hesitated, thinking. *Maybe the virus is new, or mutated. It could lie undetected in the victim's blood.*

Namah didn't seem convinced. *Still, we would have found something foreign in their blood. Viral substrates, cell wall antigens,* something.

... You seem to have a theory of your own, Doctor.

Perhaps.

Let's hear it.

Allergies.

To what?

Don't know, but it makes sense. The body is issuing an immune response to something foreign, but if there isn't a pathogen, it could be an allergen.

We've been here ten years, the refugees even longer. Why now?

Can't say, but I think it's a good place to start looking.

I hesitated, thinking again, *Very well. Refer your sickest patients to the Plexus and I'll round up my clinicians here. Once the peace ceremony is dealt with, we'll start preparing for an experimental treatment.*

Sounds fine. Talk to you soon.

I removed my finger from the rune and looked jadedly out my office window. Moritoria didn't provide much scenery—or color—but the bleak, gray world beyond was surprisingly ataractic. As calm as I acted toward Namah, the issue was very alarming.

Lucifer didn't know yet, as with everything else happening right now the last thing he needed to worry about was an epidemic. I would tell him when the time was right. If Namah and I could figure out the cause and eradicate the threat, maybe I wouldn't have to tell him at all.

I pulled out my chessboard and set up the pieces, playing against myself. The stress was almost crippling, and I needed a clear head to devise an experimental trial. Keeping part of my brain occupied with a game tended to soothe me.

Sanctum PB news was still on my televised screen. I hadn't changed it since Qaira's statement. The Nehelian broadcast station was only accessible to certain places around Heaven—never the commoners—just as Crylle news broadcasts were made available to Eroqam and Parliament. It was our way of practicing the *no secrets between us* clause of our alliance.

Nothing paramount had happened since his statement. No one had died, or been murdered. Still, I kept the channel running in case the turbulence persisted.

Most of the talk was about the peace ceremony. Apparently the Nehelians were very excited about it, already lining up at Yema Theater to access tickets to the event, even though Qaira had yet to announce it. Their want of peace made me smile.

I wondered what kind of acts Lucifer would bring to Sanctum. Angels reveled in the arts—literature, poetry, plays. Dance was mainly a Nehelian thing. I'd seen a performance of it once, and remembered how mesmerized I was by the way so many bodies moved together; some harmoniously, some completely in synch, stomping their feet to create an aggressive, alluring beat. Qaira had told me it was a war dance, practiced thousands of years ago, before one clan prevailed and formed Sanctum. He said they danced to appease Maghir, and although their beliefs often confused me, I was dazzled by his story.

That memory withered my smile.

I missed our get-togethers. Since Tae's death, nothing was the same. My only hope was that this peace ceremony would make everything right.

XVII
PIECES

THE WEEK HAD FLOWN BY IN A BLINK, spent with organizing acts, refurnishing the venue, screening potential guests, and of course, wiring demolition.

After carefully examining the blue prints, Kada suggested placing the explosives at vulnerable foundation sites which would potentially pose more damage to the angel audience, and not the Nehelians, seated on ground level. I didn't share his opinion. The house was coming down on *everyone*, regardless of where we placed those explosives. Not to mention harming mainly angels would detract all logic from an act of angel terrorism.

I tried my best not to listen to the hum of the anticipating crowd as I sat on stage, concealed by red curtain, testing my mic. Lucifer and Yahweh were already here, somewhere backstage, and Sanctum's port was teeming with angel bureaucrats, siphoning through the city on craft shuttles to Yema. The media had amassed all over the city, some reporters covering the growing crowd of protesters that had rallied near the port. More than a few people didn't want the peace ceremony. If only they knew how much that pleased me.

But no matter how hard I tried to clear my mind, guilt clenched at my insides. It made preparations difficult, not to mention the horrifying thought of having to speak to the audience *before* the carnage. On my way in I'd caught a glimpse of the crowd—families, elderly, children. That sight nearly had me dialing Kada to call the whole thing off.

But then Tae had haunted me in the rehearsal room from a full-length changing mirror. I thought of all the sleepless nights and episodes of panic; all the hopeless attempts at pulling myself together, the fights with Leid and the storming out in the middle of the night to fly aimlessly around the city.

No, this all had to end. It was the only way.

Leid had inked me the night before, the sting of the pen still fresh on my skin. Wet coua dust, the components of the ink itself, lined my eyes like war-paint. Liner was only worn on special occasions, and although the purpose behind it was akin to the battle cry of a thousand years ago, the audience would assume it was worn out of the deepest respect. Time was Tradition's archenemy.

Sound check was a success, and I slipped out of sight as the curtains drew back for the Sanctum Symphony. My brother was standing in the hallway backstage, watching dismally as crowds of media personnel begged our guards to let them through. When the ceremony began, I would place Ara and his team outside Yema to 'thwart any threats'.

"This is getting crazy," he murmured. "Pretty soon we'll need more guards. Those protestors are trying to knock over the port gate."

Good, all the more reason for Ara to go outside. "I'll admit I wasn't expecting all the hysteria."

"When do you speak?"

"After the first act."

He nodded. "Better get ready, then."

I patted him on the shoulder and headed up the stairs.

***

Lucifer sat on a couch in the rehearsal room, reading over his speech, a frown etched across his face. He seemed as nervous as me. The angel guards stepped away from the door, and Raith's eyes rose at my entrance. He was dressed in black again, a white

154

mantle draped over his shoulder. His hair was loose and hung down his back, bone straight, ice-blonde.

Yahweh was at the other side of the room, talking to a group of angel coordinators. The Commander had brought his own team to Yema. Safety in numbers.

My eyes lingered on Yahweh, the guilt growing heavier. He turned and smiled, and I looked away.

"Has it begun?" asked Raith.

"Soon," I said. "I just wanted to make sure you have everything you need."

"I do, thank you."

"Is Leid not here?" asked Yahweh.

I shook my head. "She has class, sadly."

The kid tilted his head. "I thought your schools would have closed for this."

"You and me both, but it's a weekday and she has tenure."

When Leid had told me that she wouldn't be able to make it to the peace ceremony, I didn't press the matter. It was better that she wasn't here; made everything a lot easier.

"Pity," he mumbled, stalking off.

I backed for the door, nodding at Raith. "I'm going to prepare for my speech. Good luck to you."

"Break a leg, Qaira."

I frowned, acknowledging the double-meaning behind that, and he smiled. Without another word I headed for the rehearsal room across the hall. Once there, I messaged Kada over Aeon that the detonator should be set for an hour. I wanted it to happen as Lucifer gave his speech, ensuring he was right in the middle of it all.

I looked at the mirror, sighing as Tae's grotesque, re-animated corpse stared back at me.

In only an hour, I would be free.

***

The ceremony opened with a double-act. Twelve Nehelians and angels moved together across the stage, trading batons and swords on fire. The angels sang a hymn of Moritoria while the Nehel danced aggressively to the rhythm of the war-song, and then the angels broke into a dance of quicker form.

Their bodies moved to a strange, thunderous beat, creating shapes and lines, their limbs like rubber. The music was even stranger—digitized, mechanical sounds with a melodic, sad cadence—but nonetheless impressive. Even I was drawn to watch the act from backstage. Wings Of black and white coalesced in flashing spotlights as the crowd screamed their approval. The choreographic training for this had been a nightmare.

I gave my speech after that, spouting culture and diplomacy, peppered with Archaean phrases which won me points with the angels. They clapped every time. I spoke highly of Commander Raith and our alliance, stomaching the disgust that threatened to crush my charming, calm façade. But I survived all twenty minutes of it, and had done an excellent job, too. I vacated the stage to screaming applause from both domains.

Another act prepared as the curtains drew. An angel poetry performance. I'd pass on watching that.

Raith would be up after, so it was time to gather my things.

Luckily the protestors had started throwing bottles and other garbage, injuring guards and inducing a riot. I didn't even have to order Ara outside, as he and more of his men were forced to stave them back through force. Had I been devout, I'd have said Maghir was on my side today.

In the rehearsal room again, I checked my watch. The countdown was at twenty-five minutes. In ten minutes I would greet the media, tactfully placing myself outside Yema, remaining in public view. The demolition would go off while I was speaking to Sanctum PB. No one would suspect a thing on my part. Maybe I'd up the dramatics a bit and scream for my men to save Commander Raith on live television. Yes, that would do.

I called Kada in order to verify everything was in order, because I'd noticed that he hadn't sent me a message back yet. The call looped in pending, and after a minute of no one answering, my heart began to sink.

I tried again, but still nothing.

I called the Research Science private line, hoping he'd placed his portable Aeon somewhere out of ear's reach. But no one answered that, either.

The sinking feeling transcended to full-blown panic.

Now I'd have to figure a way out of Yema unseen and fly to Eroqam. I had to find out what had happened. The private port wasn't accessible to the public, but there would be guards, and they would see me. If I left, that would leave me open for suspicion once (if) the demolition went off. My plan was falling apart, but desperation waved the danger.

The private port it was.

O
THWART

I WATCHED FROM A HOVER CRAFT AS MY soldiers tasered the frenzied mob bordering Yema, ducking bottles and flaming garbage. Some of Sanctum PB had gathered behind the gate to film the protestors, spinning a great story of rebellion. While I was slightly heartened by the sight of our people showing their allegiance to our family, speaking out against Tae's murder and Qaira's transparent want of continued peace, I was also beginning to fear for the safety of Yema's audience.

If it got any worse, we would have to cancel the ceremony. And I really hoped that happened, because—;

My Aeon chimed, and I looked down at it with trepidation.

Too late; it had already started.

Go ahead.

Commandant, said one of my men charged with guarding the private port, *the Regent just left the ceremony. Do you know anything about this?*

He was ordered back by a CA to take a call from the Plexus. He will return shortly.

An extremely weak lie, but my soldier bought it.

Swallowing the lump in my throat, I dialed Leid's frequency. My brother's abrupt departure didn't entail Communications or the Plexus, but I knew exactly where he was heading.

Leid had been right all along, and it broke my heart.

Yes?

Qaira left, I said. *He's heading your way.*

Thank you.

She severed the call, saying nothing else. Leid had wanted to be wrong, too.

"Take me to Eroqam," I ordered my pilot. He gave me a confused look, but nodded, obeying my charge.

I was about to betray my brother. Not many things in life were more painful.

But I was relieved that Leid's plan to draw him out had worked, as the issue didn't need any publicity. We would handle the matter privately, and if things got bad—*worse*—then I could spin a tale to the city. *What* tale, I had no idea yet, but it was clear that Qaira was all but gone and no one needed to know—;

Especially Commander Raith.

As we flew over Upper Sanctum, now only three minutes out, I reminisced about our childhood, our years at school, and then about my stint as Lieutenant in Qaira's Enforcers. I used to look up to him, idolize him, yearn to *be* him, but time and experience had shed some light on who he really was. My brother had always been temperamental, reckless even; but never, *never*, would he have murdered thousands of our own people. Not in his right mind, anyway.

Our sister's death had broken him. We'd known it, yet ignored it. This was as much our fault as it was his. And now we had to fix him, somehow. Hopefully Leid had an idea, because I couldn't fathom how to mend a mind capable of genocide.

I still loved him, even knowing of his plan. He was my brother, and blood ran thicker than anything, especially ours. I couldn't be too judgmental, either—I might have been just as damaged by seeing what he had.

If Qaira needed to be thrown in a psychiatric hospital for a decade, then so be it, but I could never think of executing him, even though such a crime warranted that. If the people found out, they would demand his head staked on Perula's Peak. His handsome smile and pretty words wouldn't get him out of this one.

No one could know.

No one.

XVIII
IT ALL COMES DOWN TO ONE

MY CRAFT SKIDDED INTO EROQAM'S PORT, missing the pillar by an inch. I threw open the door and lunged down the dock in full sprint.

Past the Commons and northern wing, both long-abandoned, I exploded into the science/tech wing that, albeit not abandoned, was sparsely manned. I looked at my watch, grimacing. *Ten minutes.*

Ten minutes until my window was lost forever.

The research science laboratory appeared at the end of the hall, its light bleeding through the door and into the shadowy corridor. Someone was in there.

I froze at the entrance, unable to see through its frosted glass window, curling my fingers around the handle. For the first time since I'd left Yema, I entertained the idea that someone had found out and diffused Kada's team before they could activate the demolition.

But who? Ara was at Yema, and—;

The confusion wilted away. Something in my mind clicked, and I felt my lip curl with indignation. In the seconds that had passed, fear was smothered by dark revelation. There was only one person I couldn't account for—one person smart enough to figure everything out.

I opened the door and stepped inside, bracing myself.

The research lab was quiet and inactive, save for the slow, steady hum of a generator at the back of the room. The floor was decorated with bodies of engineers, some with their necks twisted. Their lifeless eyes surveyed my entrance, laying stomach down.

A lonesome computer screen was illuminated by the image of the demolition countdown timer. It wasn't set. Beside it was Kada, knees curled to his chest, hands on his head.

Beside *him*, Leid stood with a gun against his temple. She stared at me, stoic.

Even though I had anticipated seeing her, knives still raked my heart at the thought of her knowing. I couldn't hold her gaze for more than several seconds, and cast my attention at the ground.

But Leid said nothing still, only continued to stare, a thin film of crimson tears brimming her eyes. Evidently she didn't even know what to say. I understood.

I understood because, on the outside, my plan seemed evil and psychotic. But she didn't know the truth behind it. She couldn't.

Activity from behind made me turn. My brother emerged through the door with four armed guards, rifles drawn. This I had *not* anticipated.

"On your knees," said Ara. It was a command, to me.

I looked back at Leid, shaking my head. "I...I didn't want to do this."

The sound of my voice pushed her over the edge and she let out a sob, covering her mouth.

"On your knees, Regent!" Ara shouted. *"I won't tell you again!"*

I met my brother's eyes, snarling. "I won't bend my knee to you. You'll have to shoot me first."

But I knew Ara wouldn't kill me; his look said it all.

"Come quietly," he pressed. "No one knows what you've done yet. No one might have to if you just *come quietly*."

"I can't."

I pulled out my gun, and the guards stepped back, realizing their range. Just one thought and they would all be dead. My brother didn't flinch, knowing I could never kill him, either.

He couldn't kill me and I couldn't kill him. We were caught in a net.

"Tell me why you did it."

"Lucifer has to die, Ara."

"And the cost is ten thousand Nehelians? For someone who supposedly hates him, you sure place a high value on Raith's head."

I wanted to explain it to him—to make him understand exactly *why*—but all those words had escaped me. What I said wouldn't have mattered, anyway. They thought I was insane. Maybe I was.

Massaging my head, I staggered back, feigning weakness. I dropped my gun and knelt for the ground in submission. "I'll come quietly."

Ara nodded, relieved. He ordered the guards to apprehend me. As two of them reached for my arms, another two standing at my back, I closed my eyes and their heads erupted all at once, sending blood, brain matter and skull fragments across the room.

My stagger had cleared enough distance between my brother and I, unbeknownst to him, and now he was manless, *weaponless.* He opened his mouth to shout something as I leapt backward, snatching an object off the blueprints table.

The killswitch.

Leid had moved to stop me, but her body whirred to a halt when she saw what was in my hand. They hadn't known it was here, but I'd seen it the moment I stepped inside the room. Although demolition was set with a timer, a killswitch was always instated as a failsafe in case of malfunction. The code was already set; all I had to do was push that shiny red button.

"Qaira, *no,*" she begged, her voice nothing more than a whisper.

I didn't respond, mesmerized by the switch.

Ara only stood there, panicked, hands on his head.

"Look at me," she said. *"Look at me."*

I did. She was only several feet away, her face soft and serene. "You don't want to do this."

"I don't," I said. "I don't want to do this, please believe me."

"Then give me that switch." She reached for it, slowly, *gingerly*. I watched her arm extend, my own beginning to tremble. I wanted to give it to her, I really did, but then I caught a glimpse of Tae in the window pane, her face contorted in a silent scream as dozens of black, smoke-like hands pried at her.

No.

"No," I gasped, recoiling. "Tae has to be avenged or her soul won't rest! Honor is our only decree!"

My brother and wife were left silent, their surprise mutual. Never before had I recited anything remotely devout.

"Tae would *never* want this!" cried Leid, tears threatening to fall once again. "You're not honoring your sister by committing genocide! You're staining her name!"

"You know nothing," I said through my teeth. "You know nothing of what I see, of what I know. She wants this. She told me."

Crimson beads trickled down Leid's face as she winced at those words. "Qaira, you're sick. Whatever you've seen or heard isn't your sister. It isn't, I promise. Please, let us help you. *Please.*"

I watched her cry, feeling my heart shatter into a million pieces. I thought about how it had all come to this, and knew that even if I gave her the switch, we would never be the same. Nothing would ever be the same again. I had always been a man of my word, and I had promised Tae her retribution. My lips trembled as I spoke:

"I… I'm sorry."

My thumb mashed the trigger.

The tremors of the demolition were felt beneath our feet, even from miles away. Leid sank to her knees, gripping my pantleg, encumbered by sobs. Ara was furious, screaming profanely, but I could barely hear anything in the room. It had all become a drone of slow motion as honor and shame coalesced. My conscience screamed its confusion, manifesting knives inside my head.

When it all roared back, Ara was shouting orders into his radio, and Leid was still at my feet. She wasn't crying anymore—now still and silent, head hung, face hidden by her hair. I looked back at the window.

Tae was gone, the pane revealing only the dark pillar of smoke over Yema.

Suddenly, Leid was on her feet.

Head still hung, she aimed her gun behind us and fired, nailing Ara right between the eyes. He fell instantly, the radio rolling from his hand as blood pooled around the back of his head.

I watched the blood expand, stunned.

Leid looked up at me, her hair sliding away. Black eyes, wicked smile.

"If lives are so expendable, Regent, allow me to relieve them from you. Starting with *yours*." Her voice was hollow, metallic. Fear twisted in my chest as the sound of it penetrated my senses.

She dropped the gun, and her hand exploded into a cloud of gore. A black, pincer-like scythe emerged from the severed appendage. Leid snarled, her elongated canines gleaming in the flickering lights.

Namah had called them monsters.

I was staring at the true form of a Vel'Haru, and now I knew that despite everything, Leid had never been a woman. She was a *thing*. A terrifying thing.

I bolted for the door, but she whirred in front of it and I ran right into her fist. The force of the blow sent me into a cluster of desks. My lower back tingled and the coppery taste of blood invaded my mouth. I couldn't move.

Leid clutched my boot and pulled me from the wreckage while I clawed at anything within reach. As she dragged me through Ara's pool of blood on the way to the door, I caught the doorframe, but she yanked me hard enough to dislocate my shoulders and tear several nails from their beds.

The last thing I saw was Kada, still curled on the floor beside the computer. His eyes were filled with horror.

***

I was dragged through the Commons by my foot, eyes glazing under each fluorescent light we passed.

I had no idea where she was taking me, nor did I inquire. Leid hummed a catchy tune as we went, all but skipping down the hall, like a peasant child dragging a gigantic sack of potatoes through a bustling market, excited by the prospect of a meal.

All the while I thought about Ara and the way he'd looked, lying there on the floor next to his men. In a fraction of a second he had gone from living to casualty, and the subsequent events hadn't given me any time to process that.

My entire family was dead.

Hot tears brimmed my eyes and I couldn't wipe them away. Instead I closed them and turned my head, but the floor tiles skinned the side of my face and I was forced to look upright again.

We were at the port.

Leid pulled me by our crafts, to the external hangar, and then pressed the lock disengage button. The thick sheet of steel rose painfully slow as cold wind and wailing sirens flooded in.

She stopped at the edge of the docking spire and held me on my knees by a fistful of hair. Behind us the orange glow of Yema's fire illuminated the night, and I could see its reflection in her eyes. Wind slapped my face and I squinted as she all but dangled me over an eighty-five story drop.

"You are a bastard, Qaira Eltruan," she said. "A bastard who doesn't deserve the power or world he was given. But you have my eternal gratitude." She smiled. "Without you, I might never have been free again."

"L-Leid..."

"Leid is not here anymore, sweet bastard; but don't worry, I'll take good care of you."

And with that, Calenus' warning returned.

It feeds on weakness, eating little pieces of her at a time. Soon Leid won't be able to keep it down and it will take over completely.

And then you'll die. And then your world will die. Everything it touches will die, until the Multiverse is gone.

I'd condemned Sanctum to burn.

"Let's see if those beautiful wings can save you now," Leid cooed.

She kicked me off the edge, and I fell soundlessly, staring up at her and she down at me with that horrible, wicked grin. My life flashed before my eyes—still-frame moments of better times—until I couldn't see her anymore and was drowned in torrents of violent wind and cinders.

Into the black I sank.

O
RIVEN

Yahweh Telei—;

"YOU'RE ON IN FIVE, COMMANDER RAITH," announced Tilir, Yema's coordinator. He stood at the door, glancing uneasily at the guards beside him.

"Thank you," said Lucifer, frowning.

"You're nervous," I whispered.

"No," he said, "I'm just…"

"Nervous."

The frown melted away, and he grinned. "You're distracting me. I need to go over my speech one more time."

I nodded, retreating from the couch.

My Aeon chimed. Drat this thing.

It was Namah, and although I should have found his persistence annoying, this had marked the third ring within the hour. I clipped the headset and chip behind my ear.

What is it?

Yahweh, we have an emergency.

I was startled by his greeting. *What do you mean?*

Fifty people have been rushed to Adonai with terminal emphysema. We've lost three since admittance. Doctors around Crylle have been asking for you. It's Heaven-wide.

I said nothing for a second, staring ahead. I glanced at Lucifer, who was now looking at me.

I can't do anything right now. I'm in Sanctum all evening.

You have to come back! We need as many doctors as we can get! Commander Raith has to issue a medical alert so we can contain the illness before it spreads to everyone!

... That's not for me to decide. One moment.

I removed the chip and held it out to Lucifer. He looked at it, quizzically.

"It's Dr. Ipsin," I said. "He... has news for you."

And with that, I had signed my death warrant. Metaphorically, anyway.

He took the headset and Aeon from me. After a minute or two Lucifer severed the call and grabbed my arm, ushering me out of the rehearsal room. He found Tilir in the hall on our way to the private port and told him that his speech would have to be pushed back until after the next act. As reluctant as Tilir seemed, he obliged and then once again I was tugged down the hall, pouting the entire way.

He released me at the port, and we shivered under Sanctum's winter. The sky was black and cloudless, yet flecks of snow drifted around us, salting our clothes and hair. Neither of us had brought a coat.

"People have been terminally ill for *weeks*, and you didn't tell me?" accused my father.

"None of them were terminal until now." When Lucifer only glared at me, I held out my hands. "What, would you have had me burden you with *another* problem? The conflict with Sanctum was crushing you already."

The anger on his face waned. "I appreciate your concern, but an epidemic is a burden you can't shoulder. That's my job, not yours."

"Like I said, it wasn't an epidemic until now. For all I knew it was a new strain of common cold. I already scheduled a treatment trial for next week; it's not like I was shoving the issue under the rug."

Lucifer seemed conflicted, gazing at the port door. "I shouldn't be here. I should be at Theosyne addressing the public."

"No, this is *too* important. I'll go, but you need to give your speech. It's our only shot at cementing the—"

A rumble beneath our feet stopped my mouth. As I looked down, the tremors spread from the port to Yema's wall, cracking it like an egg. Guards ran from the theater's exterior and to the docks as pieces of cement rained on us. Yema was collapsing.

Lucifer grabbed my arm and followed the guards, shielding his head with his other hand. Our wings released and we soared toward the exit as ash and white dust savaged the air. The guards' screams broke the thunder as they were crushed by fallen stones, and the sounds of their deaths brought me to the conclusion that, at any second, we'd be buried with them.

But then cold, fresh air invaded my lungs and I finally opened my eyes, looking at Yema from across the lot—caved in, on fire, collapsing further into a bed of smoking rubble.

The protestors' cries had gone from angry to terrified, and we ducked around a parking pillar as survivors stormed away from the ruins and into the arms of confused, horror-stricken patrol guards. Crafts loomed overhead, while Sanctum PB reporters projected hysteria to the masses.

I watched everything with a hand covering my mouth. Had we not been at the port, we would have been dead. Lucifer would have been in mid-speech, and—

Lucifer would have been in mid-speech.

Qaira.

I spun and gazed up at my father, who surveyed the carnage with a knowing scowl. He'd come to that conclusion much quicker than I.

"We have to get out of here," he said, hushed.

"Our crafts have b-been destroyed."

"We'll find another one. We can't be here; they'll claim us responsible."

I looked at the crowd amassing around the gate. There were few survivors, none of them angels. My stomach flipped. I felt nauseous.

"Yahweh, *come.*"

I followed Lucifer as he sought cover in the smoke.

***

Abandoned crafts were strewn across Main Street, their drivers
having left them with the keys still in their ignitions to gape at the
explosion. At Yema's collapse, everything in Sanctum seemed to
stop.

We darted from cover of the alleys and hopped inside the
closest one. Lucifer revved the craft and took flight, fumbling with
the rudimentary—if not *primitive*—controls. Qaira had told us that
he'd upgraded their crafts several years ago, and if *this* was the
upgrade, Heaven help them.

We traveled along the aeroway with our heads down as
clusters of Sanctum guards and military sped by, on the way to the
scene. Lucifer attempted to hijack the radio and connect it to his
Aeon, making it two-way transmissible, no doubt to warn
Theosyne and our militia. I had no idea what he planned to do
when we reached aerospace borders, but that was the last thing on
my mind.

Sanctum's night was advantageous, so dark that we were kept
hidden in shadows. I huddled against the passenger seat, hugging
my knees, watching lights and crafts whir by the window. "We're
abandoning those people."

"What could we have done by staying there?" asked Lucifer,
casting me a sidelong glance. "Dug them out with our hands?
We're marked."

"Are we completely sure about that?"

"One hundred percent. I would have been on stage. The timing
was too perfect. I knew Qaira was up to something…" He trailed
off, sighing. "But I never thought he'd use his own people as
props. I underestimated him. Or *overestimated* him, really."

I looked back out the window, my reflection sullen.

"We need to be out of the city before he finds out we're
alive."

"And then what?"

"Then I'll rally our troops at Theosyne and we'll march on Sanctum. Qaira will get his war."

No, not again.

"We could destroy this world with another war!" I cried. "Sanctum's technology is almost as good as ours, and the Nehel won't use the same reservation as us!"

"Yahweh, Qaira just murdered twenty thousand people—half of them angels—all to kill *me*. Do you really think this is going to end here? Do you really think that he hasn't already planned to march on Heaven the moment I was gone?"

I didn't reply, only lowered my head.

"We will march on Sanctum and overthrow its Parliament. Qaira will have a public execution, the Nehel way. No more compromises. No more negotiations. He is a genocidal tyrant who needs to be put down."

Lucifer didn't look himself while he'd said that. Seldom did he shout, and he hadn't shouted then, but his fury was detectable by the quiver in his voice and the fire in his eyes. Only twice had I seen him like this, and it was understandable. I *completely* understood his reason for war, but...

Violence and death did not cure violence and death. It was like trying to extinguish fire with fire.

As we neared the Border Patrol station, I huddled further into my seat. It was barricaded—apparently Sanctum Law Enforcement had made the executive decision to seal off the city. We were trapped.

For the first time ever, Lucifer muttered an obscenity.

We looped back to the aeroway, considering our (lack of) options.

"We need to find Leid, or Ara," I said. "If we tell them what happened, they'll believe us. I know they will."

"Even if they do, Qaira is the Regent. If he orders our execution, his brother has no choice but to exact his charge."

"He wouldn't. Not if Qaira was responsible for this."

Lucifer took a second to register what I was trying to say, tinkering again with the radio. "So, you want me to fly to Eroqam and request to see the Commandant? You want me to fly to Qaira's *house?*"

"Ara would still be at Yema."

"We're not going back there. We already ran; it would look too suspicious."

"I told you not to run."

He glared at me.

Before Lucifer could say any more, thunder broke the sky. We looked behind us, toward the silhouette of Eroqam that loomed over Upper Sanctum.

More thunder.

The western spire suddenly snapped like a twig, crushing the street below. Now there were *two* fires raging across Sanctum.

Neither of us said a thing, struggling to make sense of what just happened.

More spires fell—and then Eroqam collapsed in the same manner as Yema, a cloud of black smoke and debris billowing into the sky.

Maybe we were wrong. Maybe this wasn't Qaira's doing at all.

Sanctum was under attack. Could it have been... us?

But then the buildings on Main Street *shivered*. The air rippled as a dome of light, laden with violet sparks, enclosed the district. Flecks of supercharged matter glittered in the flow of reverse-gravity, fuzzing our craft's transmission signal.

At the sight, Lucifer floored the pedal, swerving back toward the border station. Apparently he'd decided that getting shot down by Sanctum Guard wasn't nearly as lethal as sticking around, because that was not the phenomenon of any angel or Nehelian war-machine—;

It was *Vel'Haru*, priming a field for battle.

XIX
THEORY OF ANNIHILATION

MAGHIR WAS PLAYING A CRUEL JOKE ON ME. I had survived an eighty-five story plummet into a bed of jagged coua.

Alive was an overstatement. I wasn't dead, yet hardly alive— alive just enough to watch my city disintegrate in bubbles of hot, violet light. The sight was beautiful and terrifying, but awe quickly gave way to devastation.

Bodies were strewn across the street, hundreds more fell soundlessly, like raindrops against the roar of Sanctum's end. The sky was decorated with stardust and black feathers, and my eyes closed as they brushed against my face.

My eyes yearned to stay closed. I was so tired.

So tired.

But the sound of shattering glass knocked my lids back, and I saw the strange bubbles erupt, fading in darkness and fire. Explosions rumbled the ground, and the few buildings still standing shook, shedding layers from their structure.

A body rolled through the ground-level window of a high-rise, skidding into the middle of the street.

A silhouette pursued it, and the body got to its feet.

They both became blurs, moving too quickly to see.

More blurs, more carnage, more confusing shifts in gravity that left a painful pressure in my ears. Thoughts grew less cohesive

177

and cold tingles drifted down my chest. My vision started to tunnel, and then I knew that I was dying.

I drifted to the sound of sobs, its echoes carried by the wind and flames, and my last ounce of strength had been used for recognition.

The cries belonged to Leid.

***

"Regent?"

I stirred at the whisper, emitting a croak of despair at the idea that I was *still* alive.

The pain was too much to bear, yet my body refused to give up. My heartbeat was slow, paired as it tried to pump oxygen to damaged, unrepairable organs.

I opened my eyes, staring at Calenus Karim.

He sat beside me on the coua bed, pity and sadness behind his gaze. His eyes drifted over my broken, shredded wings and shattered limbs, and then he shook his head.

"You didn't listen to me. You didn't listen to me and now here you are." Calenus looked out at the ruins of Sanctum, a proud city now nothing more than a field of smoldering wreckage. Ash flakes drifted to the ground like snow, covering the ruins in a soft, white blanket. The dead were only distinguishable by contours along the ground—tiny silo-shaped hills—and soon I would join them.

"Here you are," he said again, lowering his head. And then he laughed softly, but there was no happiness in it. "Leid will be the end of us all. She's like a vial of sweet-tasting poison, and even though we know it's poison, we still drink her. Fools, all of us."

I winced as a rattle in my chest shot fire through my lungs. Calenus put a hand on my shoulder, easing me. "When she finally snapped out of it, she begged for your life, even knowing there can be no witnesses. She begged and begged, and she has that way about her, you know. I told her you will die, and she *thinks* you will die, but alas…"

Calenus leaned in, wrapping his arms beneath my shoulders. Excruciating pain spasmed through my body and I tried to scream, but the only thing that came from my mouth was a sigh. He lifted me from the ground, lips grazing my ear.

"I am not the monster she thinks I am. Now *sleep*."

XX
REBIRTH

Purging complete.
Initiating temporal lobe activity…
Complete. Standby as resuscitation process begins…
…Loading…
…Loading…
Complete.

MY SKIN TINGLED AS COLD AIR COURSED THROUGH THE pod. The door slid open with a hiss, and the warm, soothing liquid drained away, leaving me naked and shivering in the shadowy recesses of the Nexus hive.

Everything hurt.

Aczeva watched from a stool beside the terminal, his electric eyes so bright that I had to squint against them. "Are you alright?" he asked, cautiously.

"How long was I out?"

"Five minutes on the mark. The change is already apparent."

Confused, I looked at my reflection in the pane of the pod hatch. My eyes were bright silver, ringed with crimson. Nehelian eyes—something I had lacked until now.

"H-How?" I whispered. How had the Nexus been able to hide my true appearance?

"Phenotype suppression," said Aczeva. "Your memories were gone, your heritage gone with them. Mind over matter, your Honor."

Honor.

I lowered my head, letting everything sink in. The lunacy of it all brought a twisted smile to my lips. But the smile was not a happy one—no, it was an angry one. A *furious* one; the fury so pure that all I could do was grin.

I remembered Jerusalem and the look Leid had worn once she'd unmasked me. Oh, how priceless.

"Did you find what you were searching for?" Aczeva asked as I stepped from the pod, still shivering. He handed me my clothes and I dressed, thumbing the Jury insignia across the arm of my jacket. Arbitrary it had been, only to mean so much now.

"Yes," I said, after a long silence. "Thank you."

Aczeva recited the sanitization procedure as he led me out of the hive, and I stared at the back of his head with eyes like daggers. He hadn't just given me back the knowledge of who I was, but also what I'd done while in service to the Nexus—all the worlds I'd seen, all the people I'd slain... It made my deeds as Regent seem soft by comparison.

We stepped onto the floating disc and descended to the entrance.

"What is the purpose of the Nexus?" I asked.

"The purpose?"

"The objective. Surely it has one."

Aczeva hesitated, uncertain of my meaning, but then said, "The Anakaari is an empire, and we can't run an empire without alliances and funds."

"Like Exo'daius."

Aczeva hesitated again. "Sort of. But your lot lacks an empire."

I laughed. "That's very true. And do you know what else we lack?"

As we neared the dock, he fiddled with the control panel. "What's that?"

"Mercy."

Aczeva turned to look at me, right before I kicked him off the platform. He fell into the bottomless crevice, flailing like a torch into the darkness.

The way in which the Anakaari moved—gliding, *floating* almost—made me question whether they could fly, but my fear was soothed as his screams faded.

Good riddance.

Docked, I stepped off the platform and made my way to the sanitization chamber. The group of scientists waiting at the door noticed I was chaperone-less and stepped back, concerned. They seemed even more concerned when I released my scythes.

The Nexus couldn't stand another minute, and I had the power to tear it all down. This place had much to say about the nature of the Anakaari Empire, and in return I would offer up some truth to their opinions of *God Killers*.

But my list of to-do's didn't stop there. After the Nexus burned I would return to Purgatory—;

And have a nice, long chat with my lovely, *deceitful* wife.

~*~

An angel and demon sat down for a game of chess.
One left a victor, the other defeated,
And the events that followed cost the lives of too many.

I

NEEDLES AND PINS

Lucifer Raith—;

I HURRIED FROM THE MORNING EATERY—briefcase in one hand, hot tea in the other—as Simeon pulled my craft to the entrance. Inside, I set my briefcase on the adjacent seat and opened the news journal that had been set in the basket beneath the sill.

"Looks like it's going to rain," said Simeon, and I caught the traces of a grin from the rearview mirror.

"Yes," I said, playing along. "But you know how unpredictable the weather can be."

"True enough. Really looks like rain this time, though."

But it never rained in Akkaroz. The city was enclosed in a biodome, perpetuating a synthetic gray sky and temperate climate, yet beyond the walls were lethal cold and a darkness truly indescribable. No light reached the deepest layer of Hell.

But, as always, we'd made it work.

"I'm surprised to see you today, Sim. Isn't your daughter graduating in Junah?"

"She is, sir, but that's later this evening."

"Ah. Well, good; I have a present for her in my office."

Simeon chuckled. "You don't have to do that, sir. Your donation for her tuition was more than enough."

I shook the journal at him. "But that's where you're wrong, Sim. That wasn't a donation, it was an investment. Hell always needs more doctors."

The skin around his eyes crinkled in the wake of a smile, gratitude behind his gaze. Simeon had been my driver for seventy years, and I took good care of my employees. They weren't only providing me a service, but weaving threads into the blanket of society—the blanket being infrastructure, duty, unity. After all, morale was obsolete if your subjects hated you.

Finding nothing paramount in the paper other than the usual economic disarray, I reclined in my seat and watched the scenery pass by the window—high-rises bridged by buttresses, two-tier city markets, the ever-prevalent blur of morning aeroway traffic. Here, things were steady. But only here.

Hell's governing house looked like a gothic castle, elevated from the ground by anti-gravity plates spanning two miles in diameter. I spent ten hours a day in a tiny glass box, pushing paper and enduring hours-long meetings with other ruling members of the Obsidian Court. I'd been in office for more years than I had not, whether be it for Heaven or Hell, and had long forgotten what it felt like to do anything else.

Lunch came far too quickly. I'd had yet to review Naberius' budget proposal for Lochai, which needed to be done by the end of the day. His layer was sinking, and I was dreading that meeting with him tomorrow.

My office Aeon chimed right as I was about to leave, and I stared at it, tilting my head. No one ever called now. Everyone knew my schedule.

I answered the call, but before I could even speak, someone said:

I'm so sorry to call you here. You know I wouldn't call you here if it wasn't an emergency.

I hesitated, surprised. I'd thought it was my secretary, but the voice belonged to Lilim, Samnaea's handmaiden. We'd been close once. Or twice.

Our brief affair had had a few perks, one being a constant flux of information from Junah's head estate.

It's alright. What's the matter?

It's happened again.

I sighed. *How long?*

Two days, sir. She won't let anyone in her room. The Aeon is ringing off the hook and I don't know what to say. I'm surprised you haven't heard about it yet.

So much for lunch.

I'm on my way. Don't tell her.

I couldn't, even if I wanted to.

Four days ago my second general, Caym Stroth, left Akkaroz without a trace. No one had heard from him since. After a thousand inquiries across Hell, it was safe to say he'd left The Atrium altogether. Though a code violation in itself, I had an idea that Samnaea knew where he was—or, judging by what Lilim just told me, what had happened to him.

The Jury had confiscated that list of Sanguine Court members before I was able to see it, but recent activities led me to believe that both of them were at the top. And that was a hard truth to swallow, especially after Samael. However Yahweh had requested to meet, claiming he could shed some light on all of this, so for the meantime I'd put my assumptions on ice.

I locked my office and informed my staff that I was going to lunch. Simeon drove me to Akkaroz's cephalon, swearing to tell no one, and I slipped inside undetected and took the portal to Junah.

Hopefully Lilum thought to call a driver.

***

The Soran estate floated on an island above Junah, with two arching spires that always reminded me of robotic arms. Chains the length of city blocks and width of pillars hung from them, their use still lost on me after all these years.

Samnaea was *expressive,* among other things. I was afraid to ask about the chains, since she'd probably delve into a lecture about the symbolism of the Ring War. Of everyone, she carried the most scars, and not all of them skin deep.

The digital clock tower at the center of the city told me that I only had thirty-five minutes left to convince Samnaea to return to work. The numbers flashed as the hour turned, leaving a hazy, blue glow across the sky, like moonlight.

Junah was the sixth layer of Hell—cold and dark, but not cold and dark enough to warrant a biodome. The scenery was perpetual night, little vegetation, with buildings etched from tundra plateaus and jagged gorge-side cliffs. Most of the citizens wore luminance-enhanced spectacles, the lenses like high-definition cameras that made it impossible to see the wearer's eyes. We called them dark glasses. People got creative with them, crafting embroidered frames or eccentric shapes. Dark glasses were the one thing that never went out of style around here.

It turned out Lilum had thought to call a driver, and he'd handed me a pair of dark glasses on the way to his craft. I took them off when I reached the estate, as warm light bled through the crack in the front door when Lilum came to greet me. She bowed, almost dramatically. I watched her silky, rust-colored hair slide over her shoulders. With eyes the color of molten steel and skin the smoothest ivory, it was hard to resist pursuit. But I wasn't here for that. Twenty-five minutes was not enough time, anyway.

"Sir, thank you so much for coming."

"Thank *you* for telling me, Lili."

Lilum looked up at me, and I could tell that she hoped I would pursue her as well. She was going to be disappointed. "Right this way."

The estate was lavish with abstract paintings and glass furniture. I didn't particularly think glass furniture was a safe form of décor—given its owner—but I kept my opinions to myself.

She led me up the winding staircase and down the black-carpeted, second floor hallway. Samnaea's bedroom lay at the end of the hall. It was locked, just as Lilum had said.

I pressed my ear to it, waving the servant away with a nod in thanks. Alone, I knocked softly.

190

"Samnaea?"

Silence.

"Samnaea, I just want to talk to you. Can you please open the door?"

I heard the soft tapping of footsteps. I pressed my ear to the door again, feeling a slight resistance this time. She had her hands against it.

"Go away."

Her voice was coarse, dry, *weak.*

"Can I remind you of the offense for telling the Commander of Hell—*your* boss—to go away?"

"I don't want to talk to anyone."

"That's a lie. Open the door."

Her footsteps padded away. I sighed.

"Samnaea, if you don't open the door, then I'm going to break it down."

"I'll explode your head."

"No, you won't. I'm going to count from five."

Silence, again.

"Five, four, three—"

The lock unlatched with a *click.* I pushed the door open, finding Samnaea in the center of the room. Her back was turned as she wiped her tears away. Boxes of documents were strewn across her bed, loose sheets littered the floor.

"What are you doing?" I asked.

"Digging. Research."

"Research for what?"

Instead of replying, she sank to the bed and held her face. My eyes trailed over the fresh scabs on her arms. She was a masochist, but that was no secret. She'd explained once that her pain was so deep, the only way to release it was to cut it from her body. Both Caym and Samael had tried to convince me to stop her on numerous occasions, but who was I to stop her? She wasn't causing fatal harm to herself, only little incisions no deeper than her skin, and if it made her feel better—*saner*—why stand in the way?

191

There were more cuts than usual, though, and that caused a twinge of sadness in my chest. Samnaea was renowned for her beauty. Undisputed, she was the most beautiful demoness in all of Hell, and the sight of those cuts even hurt *me* a little.

We went back a long way, she and I; never intimate, but always close.

And although right now she was certainly unfit for office, these episodes were seldom. Most days she was charismatic and charitable, pouring her talents of economics and diplomacy into her job. And it showed. Despite her layer being the weakest in terms of resources, she had transformed a frozen, desolate rock into a flourishing city of technology and academia. Junah found its success within the medical and scientific spectrum. Samnaea Soran was too important to lose.

"I've done terrible things, Lucifer," she whispered. "Terrible, *terrible* things. Saying them out loud will make you hate me." Fresh tears streamed down her face, and she hung her head to hide them.

Here it was; her confession. I closed the door behind me and sat next to her on the bed. Although I didn't respond, my look was enough to make Samnaea feel safe. Yet as calm as I seemed, my pulse was throbbing in my ears as I braced myself for her betrayal.

***

As Samnaea sobbed on the floor, I placed my hand on her shoulder, feeling the chill of her skin.

I tried to hide my anger, but knew she could see it. She was crying out of loss, guilt, and the fact that she'd practically crushed my heart with only a few long-winded sentences.

"I'll see you tonight," I whispered, getting up to leave.

She said nothing, only sobbed harder.

I closed the door behind me and made my way down the stairs. Lilum found me in the foyer.

"Did it work?" she whispered, casting a worried glance at the second floor.

"Lady Soran will be returning to work tomorrow, but I'm giving her one more day to collect herself. Please see to it that she has everything she needs until then."

Lilum bowed again. "Yes, sir. Thank you, sir."

The overuse of *sir* always made me cringe.

"No," I said, opening the door. "Thank *you*."

On the return flight to Junah's cephalon, I thought about my next move. The dark, ominous scenery served a fitting ambiance.

Political machinations were never my thing. Unfortunately the Sanguine Court had to be eliminated, and now I had the proper fuel for that fire.

II
REPERCUSSIONS

Lucifer Raith—;

"DO YOU remember Day Zero?"

I hesitated, studying Samnaea as she sat cross-legged on the floor of my study, cradling a cup of hot cider. She awaited my response, eyes large and bright like liquid gold.

"Of course I do."

She smiled sadly, staring into her steaming beverage. "Thousands of us stumbling through the ruins of Sanctum, scared and excited, sifting through our losses and gains."

Day Zero was the first day that the demons had migrated to Hell. Back then our home was nothing more than seven layers of tundra and endless fields of ice, so we'd had no choice but to seek shelter in Sanctum, then centuries lost. The angels had shuttled us down here in transporter crafts, prodding us out like cattle, leaving us shivering in darkness.

I didn't know how to respond. The mentioning of Sanctum left a bitter taste in my mouth, which then left me vulnerable to thoughts of Justice Alezair Czynri.

Qaira Eltruan.

How Leid had found him was a mystery; we had all thought that he was dead. I wasn't yet afforded any time to pull Leid aside

195

and ask just what the hell she was doing, as his appearance had coincided with our political disarray. But I planned to. *Soon.*

For now I had to believe that he wasn't a threat, as his memories were still in safe-keeping at the Nexus.

"And now here we are," Samnaea went on, shattering my thoughts. "Millions strong, yet still we wear these invisible shackles. Why?"

"There aren't any shackles."

"But there are. I wear a dozen of them as we speak. Shackles of poverty, shackles of rapidly decreasing resources, shackles of imminent starvation, shackles of our pointless Contest... Do you know what I would give to see Heaven's sun again?"

"Let's stop traipsing down Irrelevancy Lane. Tell me about the next Sanguine Court meeting."

"It's tonight," she said, lowering her gaze. "I was supposed to attend."

"What time?"

Samnaea glanced at the clock. "An hour from now."

"Where?"

"Avernai."

I bristled. "Does Malphas know?"

She shook her head. "His underlings do, though. The meeting is being held at the governing house after hours. A secretary will be there to unlock the door."

The Sanguine Court was a syndicate of cleverly-placed seeds throughout Hell's legislature, preying on the poverty-stricken to illicit tallies through code violations. Although Samnaea had informed me that neither her brother nor partner were part of it, *she* was, along with a handful of other Archdemons whom she'd refused to name.

But that was fine. I'd find them out soon enough.

I grabbed my coat from the hangar, while Samnaea blinked at me.

"Well then, we better get moving," I said.

"Wait." She tilted her head. *"What?"*

I grinned. "Tonight I'll be your surprise guest of honor."

"No, you can't," she gasped, moving to stop me. "If they find out I've snitched, then—"

"You don't have to worry about that. Not after tonight."

Her fright switched to confusion. "… What are you planning to do?"

"I plan to remind everyone of who's in charge around here, and I need your help."

Samnaea hushed, looking conflicted.

"Since when are you afraid of anyone?" I said, near whisper. "You think a little thought and all of your enemies march themselves off cliffs."

"I'm not afraid of them. I'm afraid of *you*."

"Me?"

"I want your word that there won't be any repercussions."

I smirked, heading for the foyer. "You'll have more than my word, believe me. Come, or else we'll be late."

***

I didn't call a driver when we reached Avernai. Samnaea's confession had left me paranoid, with good reason. Word of my being here might get out if security was tainted, and I had no doubt that it was.

Instead we walked ten blocks from the cephalon to Avernai parliament, taking back roads and alleys through the city. The streets were clear, as Avernai enforced a curfew due to high crime and murder rates.

The first layer of Hell suffered worst of all, decorated in eroded buildings well past due for repairs, abandoned houses, piles of garbage and hordes of homeless.

Malphas Tremm, Avernai's Archdemon, was left floundering as his citizens migrated to other layers, taking jobs and taxes with them. Despite our best efforts to replenish Avernai's capital, the only people left were those financially incapable of migration fees, members of drug and prostitution crime rings, and the feeble minded unable to care for themselves, left to rot on the streets.

Being here and seeing it all was another bag entirely. Hell was collapsing, layer by layer, the effect like dominos. Although right now I was grateful for the abandoned streets, I was also well aware that our lives would be in danger should we run into the wrong type of people, regardless of our titles.

Something had to be done, but I could only pluck one thorn at a time.

"I should have worn a different coat," whispered Samnaea, her heels clicking loudly as she walked. "I'm sure every dredge here thinks my pockets are stuffed full with money."

"We're almost there."

"We're still three blocks away."

"A much shorter distance than ten."

She clicked her tongue, pulling the hood of her scarlet petticoat over her head in effort to conceal her face.

"So what were those boxes in your bedroom?" I asked.

"Research, like I said."

"For the Sanguine Court?"

"No, for me."

"Care to share?"

"Belial Vakkar."

When she said nothing else, I looked down at her with a curious tilt of my head. There had always been bad blood between them, but she'd never gone this far. "What about him?"

"I acquired copies of Tehlor's transactions for the past three fiscal periods. The taxes that Belial is paying to the Obsidian Court don't match the taxes he's receiving. He's embezzling money."

"And how did you get your hands on Tehlor's financial records?"

She smiled coyly through the shadows of her hood. "I have my ways."

"Mm."

"I've also found receipts of transactions from the Celestial Court."

That almost made me halt. "Say again?"

"Belial is taking payments from the Jury. He's an informant."

I exhaled, not wanting to think about that right now. Samnaea didn't take the hint.

"He's been keeping the Jury in the loop. I understand not all of our activities have been... *clean,* but the fact that he's bribable shows his level of fealty to our Court."

"And what sparked such a witch hunt?"

Samnaea looked away, watching a pile of trash burn; shadowed figures in rags were huddled around it. "I was trying to find out who tipped the Jury off to the manifest. I have no doubt it was him."

"I thought your brother gave the Justice Commander that list?"

"Belial made its existence apparent. She got her dirty claws into my brother and threatened my impeachment if he didn't hand it over."

"And how did *he* know about it?"

"Belial told him, too. Isn't that peculiar?" She let that question hang for a moment, and I had to admit that I was intrigued. "Why would he tell Leid *and* Samael? Whatever the cause, it certainly stirred some shit. Now my brother is dead; Caym, too. Not to mention the angels have tightened our noose."

There was something about the look in her eyes that told me Samnaea wasn't relaying everything she knew, but I let it slide. For now.

The twin spires of Parliament came into view across the street, wrapped in steel-knitted barbed wire. We paused, surveying the guard station. There were no patrol units, but a lone guard stood watch from the tiny glass cubicle near the entrance. Convenient.

Too convenient.

"Do you think he knows about the meeting?" I whispered.

"Of course he does. Who do you think let everyone in?"

"Pity. I'll need your expertise, then."

"...Should I kill him?"

"No, no murder, please. Just make him fall asleep or something."

Samnaea nodded, and together we crossed the street.

I waited by the gate while she strolled up to the cubicle, striking conversation. I couldn't hear what was said, but then Samnaea leaned in and the guard slumped in his chair. She waved a hand in front of his face, verifying unconsciousness, and then beckoned for me.

As we ducked under the median, I caught a glimpse of the guard. His eyes, nose and ears were bleeding. *"Samnaea."*

"He's not dead," she assured, smiling. "He'll just have a nasty migraine for a couple of days."

Sometimes she even sounded like him.

Of all the potential traits, she'd acquired Qaira's *brain apoptosis*. If only he knew of the legacy that he'd left.

Arguably Samnaea was more powerful than he'd ever been, as her ability was much more specialized. Mind control was a weapon with no equal.

Rotating cameras atop the guard station followed our movements, but given the occasion I doubted anyone was on surveillance duty. We would have to do something about them later on.

The winding stone walkway to the entrance was vacant. Lamps oscillated over the front steps, covering us in shimmering, gold light. I stepped out of sight as Samnaea at the glass double-doors. A figure was at the front desk, head down, reading something over.

She knocked.

The figure stood and slowly made their way to the door. It was Dia, Malphas' secretary. She released the lock and Samnaea stood back as the doors opened.

And then I stepped into view.

Dia's eyes widened and she tried to shut the doors again, but I barged through and held them open, snarling. Before she could run, Samnaea took hold of her mind and forced her on bended knee.

"D-Don't kill me," whispered Dia, trembling. "Please, sir, don't kill me."

I stepped aside, gesturing to the entrance. "This is your only chance to flee. Tell no one, or I will find you and have you executed for treason."

"I don't think that's wise," Samnaea murmured, leaning in.

I ignored her.

"Yes, I promise! I'll tell no one!" Dia squeaked.

"Release her," I said.

Samnaea did so, and without another word the frightened secretary bolted through the doors, fleeing into the night. She'd even left her purse on the desk.

"We should have killed her," said Samnaea, watching her retreat.

"That's not how I do things."

"I guarantee she'll snitch to anyone who'll listen."

"And who is that? Her boss has no idea of her activities, not to mention after tonight, no one will care to listen anyway."

Samnaea shot me a look. "I suppose you have a plan all figured out."

I grinned. "Of course I do."

"Why didn't you just order your guards to bust the meeting?" she asked. "I don't really understand what we're doing here."

"Guards are too impersonal."

"So you're taking this personally?"

"Why wouldn't I?" I asked, casting her a venomous look. "Members of *my* court are attempting to usurp my rule. They're coercing my people into doing horrendous things—things of which I stand against completely. They're making Hell a dangerous, ugly place, Samnaea."

"And what exactly are you doing to make Hell a less dangerous and ugly place?"

My voice caught in my throat. All I did was glare at her.

"The Sanguine Court formed because *you* aren't doing anything. Hell is collapsing and you haven't taken any steps to keep us from sinking with it." As I stood there, stunned, she pulled a malay cigarette from her bag and lit it, fouling up the air. "At least they keep the tallies in our favor, so we aren't facing slavery, too."

The poor, *poor* girl. She had no idea that the Contest was a farce. There had never been an agreement to compete for re-slavery. All Yahweh and I had done was bade time for blood. But time was running out.

"Come on," I muttered, heading for the hall. "We can talk about this later."

Other than the lobby, Avernai Parliament seemed abandoned of staff. The halls were decorated in paintings, mock-oil lamps and modern, black grate wall shelves that held memorabilia of political achievements. This city was the oldest, built directly over Sanctum, and it showed.

Every layer was unique, all depending on the Archdemon who ruled it. Each layer was a territory, and over time the need of identity generated cultures, even dialects. Avernai's theme was much more classical than Junah or Akkaroz, having placed a heavy emphasis on old-Crylle architecture. The pillars and statues outside the governing house reminded me of Theosyne, and thoughts of Heaven always left me melancholic.

Soft, orange light bled through the cracks from the council room at the end of the hall. The murmur of conversation filled my ears, and I noticed Samnaea was losing her nerve. She'd strayed behind several paces, staring at the light with trepidation.

I stopped and look over my shoulder.

"Are you sure you want to see?" she asked.

"See what?"

"*Them.* You're going to be surprised, and possibly hurt."

I said nothing and gestured for her to enter first. Samnaea sighed and lowered her head, moving through the door. The conversation turned into heated demands of why she was so late. I could already recognize a few of their voices. Before Samnaea could respond, I appeared in the threshold, and their demands turned to silence.

My eyes swept across every guest seated at the rectangular table, stopping at the end. Betrayal built to anger at the identity of their leader.

Vetis Cull.

He'd been thrown out of office half a century ago for sedition, infamous for rallying citizens against their Archdemons. Fanatical yet charismatic—Vetis was never charged of any crimes because his protests were always nonviolent. Until now.

Thinking back, I should have suspected him sooner, but the Sanguine Court wasn't his modus operandi. Whatever the reason, Vetis's psychotic vision of seizing Hell would end tonight.

Almost a minute passed; no one said a thing. Samnaea inched to the side of the door, smoking her cigarette, eyes cast to the ground.

I moved across the room until I towered over Vetis, who cowered in his seat. Never a brave man when it came to facing his dues, more the type to mutter insults at your back. The other members saw this, undoubtedly, and their silence held.

"I'm sorry to interrupt your meeting," I said, and he finally dared to meet my gaze. His eyes were like malachite, flecks of amber peppering each iris. The crimson rings around them seemed black in comparison. "Please, by all means, *continue*."

"L-Lucifer, I—"

"None of you have anything to say?" I interjected, looking around the table. "Because your actions have a lot to say. Not only has your sense of absolution placed all demons under persecution by the Celestial Court, but you've nudged us on the brink of a war that we're not ready to fight."

The members—among them Azazel Lier of Orias, Mastema Tryess of Lochai—all looked at the table like scolded children. I'd expected them to be a little more gallant. Pity.

Then again, I'd stolen Samnaea's loyalty. Without her, they were powerless against someone like *me*.

Vetis didn't try to speak again. All he did was sit there, staging a pathetic attempt at placidity. "Go on," I said to him. "Recite our decree."

Reluctant, he only shook his head.

I removed the gun from my coat pocket and pressed the barrel against his temple. The *hiss* of its charger made Vetis flinch, and his hands trembled on the table's surface. No one else said a thing, yet their shame escalated to fear.

This wasn't exactly my modus operandi, either. But drastic times called for drastic measures.

"U-Unity and peace among the citizens of Hell," stammered Vetis, his courage all but gone as the cold metal brushed against his skin. A bead of perspiration trickled from his hairline. "Protection from harm, shelter from cold, edify—"

I pulled the trigger, and Vetis slumped over. A third of his head was gone and blood flowed from the still-smoking exit wound, running like a river down the table.

I looked over the horrified crowd, cocking my gun. *"Run."*

The other demons scattered, fleeing the meeting room, the thunder of their feet heard all the way down the hall. Samnaea lingered in the doorway with a hand clasped over her mouth. Her cigarette had burned out a while ago, now just an arch of ashes threatening to fall from the filter at any moment.

Pocketing the gun, I headed for the door. Samnaea flinched, cowering against the frame.

I shot her look. "Don't be silly. Let's go."

"Where?"

"The security room. I need to confiscate those tapes and deactivate the feed."

Samnaea pointed at Vetis' body. "What about *him?*"

"That'll send a message to the others, loud and clear."

She said nothing else, following me to the basement elevator. I caught her look from the corner of my eye, knowing that she viewed me in a new light. Prior to this moment, I was never pictured in blood-splatter. The Fall had changed everything, especially how I dealt with traitors.

And the look in Samnaea's eyes wasn't fear, but respect. Dominance and aggression were attractive qualities to our kind—it was scary how close we'd grown to our predecessors. The *cure* had done much more than altered our appearance.

The elevator doors opened with a soft *ding*, and we stepped into the cool, lightless corridor. As I suspected, the security floor was vacant. Easy as pie.

***

"No, no murder please. That's not how I *do things,"* mocked Samnaea as we hurried back to the cephalon. *"I'll just shoot my cousin in the head, that's all."*

"Second cousin."

I burrowed into my scarf, thankful for the darkness that hid the blood on my coat. But I probably could have dragged Vetis' near-decapitated body through the streets in broad daylight and not a single person would have batted an eye. Just another day in Central Avernai.

"And what will you do now?" she asked, stepping over a drunken homeless man lying in the middle of the alley.

"Not sure," I admitted.

"You should have killed the others. They might come back for you. For *me*."

I laughed under my breath. "Always so quick to kill. For someone who's feared across Hell, you sure have quite a bit of it yourself."

"At the very least they could tell the press."

"Tell them what? That I came busting through the doors of their secret meeting and murdered their leader? Sounds like good PR for me. Uttering a word of this would ruin their careers, and they know it. They've learned their less—"

Something caught my eye.

A figure huddled near a cluster of waste bins, shadowed by a looming sill.

I froze, and so did Samnaea.

"Lucifer?" she asked, confused.

I didn't respond, approaching the waste bins.

205

It was the corpse of a little girl; near-naked, bones jutting from her skin. She had died alone in a slow, painful process of starvation. I imagined her curling against the trash in a last attempt to keep warm, shaking and crying as her body finally gave up. Her dead, glazed eyes relayed such hopelessness.

I looked away, swallowing hard.

Samnaea took my side, gazing down at the girl, stoic. "There are a dozen of these every day. Avernai and Lochai have started bringing out sanitization crafts to haul bodies away every morning. Where have you been?"

That was an excellent question, and I didn't know the answer.

But one thing was clear: this couldn't be about keeping peace anymore. I couldn't place a transparent alliance over the lives of my people.

Not anymore.

I turned away, tossing Samnaea my gun. She caught it, startled.

"Congratulations," I muttered, vacating the alley. "You just became my General."

III
CHECKMATE

Lucifer Raith—;

THE TEMPLE OF MAGHIR RUINS, MORITORIA.

Crumbled pillars lay beneath a thick blanket of fog, swirling around the stone plateau on a floating isle. Stardust glittered in the air, never rising nor falling, suspended by pockets of warped gravity. Moritoria marked middle ground for The Atrium— Purgatory just an island away—and here I traveled every few months to strip away my title.

Here, I regressed.

I cleared the fifty feet from ground to plateau, folding my wings when I landed. The cure had painted my hair and wings black, my Archaean traits all but gone. *Fallen*, some called us. *Demons*, others said.

Nehel, everyone knew, but wouldn't dare speak it.

Yahweh was already seated at the stone bench, setting pieces across the chessboard. At my approached, he turned and nodded solemnly. Seldom did he smile anymore.

Clad in a black business suit and powder-blue tie, he was a long shot from the boy I'd raised. A young man now, forced to lead the Argent Court and rule over Heaven, time and events had snatched all geniality from him. Sad, but inevitable.

And I was proud of him, still.

"You're late," he said as I took a seat at the table.

"I'm always late."

"You're later than usual. Trouble?"

"I wouldn't even know where to begin."

Yahweh gave me a thin smile, but didn't press. Instead he made his move: white pawn to F3.

I slid a black pawn to C5.

We had played chess thousands of times since our separation, but never before had I scrutinized his methods. Yahweh had no idea how much *this* game mattered, but he would.

"So," I said, reclining as he mulled over his next move, "you told me you had news."

Yahweh sighed, dismissing my inquiry with a wave. "One moment."

Pawn to G5.

"Caym Stroth died in Atlas Arcantia," he said then. "He was involved in a scheme to kill Leid Koseling; revenge for Samael Soran."

I stared at him, stunned, fingers hovering over a bishop. "Atlas Arcantia? That's not even—"

"Yes, I know. When I confronted the Jury about it, they told me..." He paused, worry in his gaze. "Leid told Samael about a statue that she'd hidden in Atlas Arcantia. Word of the statue got to Caym, and when she tried to correct her error and destroy it, your demons pursued her."

A statue.

At the mentioning of that, my face fell. Yahweh needn't explain.

"Calenus promised that the statue was destroyed; the threat of the Scarlet Queen gone. That's the *only* reason why Leid was selected for Justice Commander."

"You don't have to tell me. I was there; I know."

Exiled from the Court of Enigmus, Leid had returned to The Atrium seven hundred years ago to salvage a life lost to tragedy. But the life she'd had was gone; the world she'd known changed forever. The Ring War had just ended and talk of a demon-angel alliance was in the midst. Her re-appearance was fortuitous, and we'd offered her and her guardians a job of playing mediators of the Contest. In return she was granted asylum in The Atrium.

Calenus had assured us that the statue was gone and Leid could never pose another threat. None of what had happened to Sanctum was her fault, not entirely—yet just the same a disease never *chose* to infect anyone. It simply did.

And now the horrors of our past were re-surfacing all at once. Dead Vel'Haru queens, Qaira Eltruan—there was a hidden meaning in all of this, but I couldn't find it.

Bishop to H6.

"Caym was killed by Leid, then?"

"No, Alezair Czynri."

"… He was with her?"

"Yes."

She'd taken Qaira to the site of the dead queen's statue? Dangerous, dangerous, *dangerous…*

"Alezair didn't claim to kill him. He said Caym's head exploded."

My stare trailed off. "So, he remembers?"

"No, not that I could tell."

"But then how—?"

"Your guess is as good as mine."

Neither of us knew how to handle the situation. While our shock at *Alezair Czynri's* employment was mutual, we couldn't simply demand to know how Leid had found him or how he was still alive. We couldn't demand that she remove him from The Atrium, either. Instead we were forced into faking normalcy, meanwhile the former Regent of Sanctum walked around with his melon scraped out. Any inquiries would have had him asking questions, and while it was apparent that he didn't pose a threat right now, should he ever *remember…*

"The good news is that the statue has been destroyed, for real this time. One threat averted, hooray."

I said nothing, lost in thought.

For a while we played wordlessly, and soon half of our pieces were absent from the board.

After my queen murdered his knight, I said, "Out with it."

"I'm sorry?"

"You're not telling me something. I know that face anywhere."

Yahweh stared at the chessboard, deciding his next move, stalling for time. "Leid was having an affair with Samael."

My jaw practically hit the table. "How do you know?"

"She told me. His attack in Najudis was driven by heartache. He thought she'd betrayed him."

"This is becoming a circus."

"True enough. But I'm left without options. Samnaea knows, and if word gets out, we'll have to stage a punishment—"

"Word won't get out."

Yahweh lifted a brow. "You're certain?"

"Yes."

Because if she hadn't told me, then she wouldn't tell anyone. Yet now I knew of all the things she'd left out of her confession last night, and found myself wishing back that ignorance.

Yahweh looked at me, awaiting his turn. The scar across his eye never got easier to take in, and always made me reminisce about the day that he'd received it— the day he'd lost half his sight, and his innocence. *The day I'd fallen.*

My queen slid across the board, taking his bishop. He took my rook. A gallant play.

"You don't seem as upset as I thought you'd be," he murmured, wiping hair from his eyes. "I was really dreading this talk."

"Hard to surprise me these days."

"Mm."

More game, less chatter. The board was practically barren, and I was impressed. Yahweh had never survived a match this long, and the odds were even.

The next move took a while to figure out, the *tick tick tick* of the timer like a tiny drum inflecting my thoughts. Yahweh had

212

been tactful in the placement of his final pieces, to the point where almost any move I made was suicide. I looked at him with silent admiration, and he caught my drift, grinning.

"You've been practicing alone?"

"No."

"Well, you're suddenly giving me a run for my money."

"Perhaps I was always this good."

"You? *Deceptive?*" I raised my brows. "Please."

Although Yahweh had been joking, I hoped that he wasn't.

He leaned into his hand, sighing. "The timer's almost up. Stop dancing around the bush and kill me already."

Kill me already.

Kill me.

That sentence looped around my mind, and I stared at him, conflicted. My search for sympathy only turned up memories of the dead child in Avernai. I saw her in the reflection of Yahweh's eyes—even the cloudy, useless one. He and his people spent their days in sunlight, without fear of famine or cold. As empathetic as he was, there was no way that he could understand our plight. Not the way that he needed to.

And part of that was my fault. I'd made our bed half a millennium ago, unable to foresee how short that straw really was. Back then I was protecting him. But clearly he didn't need my protection anymore.

I lowered my gaze, sliding a piece across the board.

"Check mate," Yahweh said, near whisper. He looked confused by it—brows furrowed in question of whether or not I'd let him win. But I hadn't.

He was finally ready.

"The Contest is over," I stated, and his confusion intensified. "I'm declaring war on Heaven. The official declaration will be broadcasted tonight, but I wanted to give you a heads up."

I couldn't meet Yahweh's gaze, casting my attention to the board. He didn't speak for a long time.

The timer sounded off, and I silenced it with a slap.

"W-Why...?" he asked, stammering.

"That question tells me of your naivety. The Contest won't hold, Yahweh. Our resources are drying up. Demons are dying, and my own Court is attempting to usurp me because I haven't—*can't*—do anything about it. We've already tried the diplomatic route, but your Court won't go forward with allowing us more territory. They want us dead, *gone*, so that they can finally live without any mementos of their failings."

He had flinched several times during my explanation. "I... I don't feel that way."

"I know you don't," I said, guilt creeping through the cracks of my stoic façade. This was harder than I thought it'd be. "And you've done everything you can, but it's not enough. The only way your angels will ever agree to forfeit their paradise is through war."

The sadness and confusion on Yahweh's face began to wane, anger filling up the empty space. "War is not the answer. You're trying to solve your problem of death by *more* death? Resolve famine by creating nuclear wastelands? Have you gone *completely* insane?"

Yahweh's inability to see reason left me cold. Ignoring his slander, I left the table. "In a month's time we will be marching on Heaven. If you know what's good for you, you'll take the necessary precautions to defend your land accordingly."

He shot up as well, smacking the board off the table. Pieces scattered across the plateau, and I watched them roll away, not bothering to fetch any—;

Because I knew that this had been our last match. Now we would play for real.

"No!" he shouted. *"I won't let you do this! You can't do this! We made a promise that war would never happen again! Stop walking away! Stop walking away and face me!"*

My wings unfolded and spread. I paid him a single glance over my shoulder. "War is coming, whether you want it or not. Good luck with whatever you decide, Yahweh Telei."

I lifted off, ignoring his shouts at my back. But as frigid as I'd been, there was an aching deep inside, perpetuated by guilt. My poor son; he couldn't see the hurt in my eyes as I flew away.

Visions of everlasting peace had deluded him, yet the inevitability of this moment was a century-coming.

I was not his father anymore, but his adversary.

And hopefully he would come to terms with that soon enough.

IV

EMBERS

Belial Vakkar—;

THE STAGE LIGHTS WERE PERFECT, AS WERE the prop designs and costumes. Aesthetically this production couldn't have been better, but any talented playwright knew a theatrical presentation couldn't coast on visuals alone.

And that was exactly the case here. My actors couldn't hold a line to save their lives, their movements clumsy and overcompensating. I wasn't even watching anymore; instead I stared at a close-up view of my palm as it covered my face.

"Oh my god, cut," I sighed.

No one heard me.

The Maiden stuttered her next line, and the Bear tripped over his own feet. The costume had been designed for someone bigger, but my first choice was in critical care after having his skull fractured by a flying punchbowl during that brawl at my masquerade. I had a half a mind to sue the Jury for the revenue I was certainly going to lose, and I'd have sued Samael Soran too, but he was dead.

"Cut!" I shouted, and this time everyone heard me. They froze; the music stopped. "What the bloody hell was *that?* Am I directing an elementary school performance?"

"I can't keep my lines straight if Dreisel won't keep his!" Alina the Maiden exclaimed. The Bear, played by my servant and

217

usually-talented actor Dreisel, ripped off the head of his costume, tossing it on the floor. His face was drenched with sweat.

"Master Belial, I'm suffocating in that thing! Can't we use make up, or even glue some ears to my head?"

"Just take five," I hissed, unable to deal with them any longer. As Alina and Dreisel continued to have at it, I retreated backstage, debating whether to call the whole thing off. But I'd poured so much money into it already—even if the production sucked, at least I could gain a little money back. The only dilemma here was the idea of staining my reputation for revenue.

Well, not like that hasn't happened before, but still.

I found solace in the rehearsal room, sinking into a swivel-chair. Staring at my reflection, I pulled a malay cigarette from the pack in my breast pocket. My reflection showed a tired man, in desperate need of rest. Archdemon of Tehlor by day, playwright and director by night. Sleep was for the dead.

I closed my eyes and fantasized about my bed—the way the sheets felt across my skin, the softness of the pillow. My Aeon vibrated in my jacket, jolting me awake. I had to get out of this bloody chair before I fell asleep.

I held the cigarette in my mouth, squinting against the smoke while pulling the Aeon up to my face. A frequency flashed across the screen. It was Persephone.

I glanced at the clock over the door. It was an hour and a half past the time I'd promised to be home. This production wasn't boding well for anyone.

I left the rehearsal room and headed for the alley-side exit, hoping some cold air would wake me up. The entire trip I debated answering Persephone's call. If I did, I'd hear an earful. If I didn't, I'd hear an earful when I got home. Better now than later.

Hello, my dear.

Don't you 'my dear' me. Where are you?

Still at Garivel. So sorry.

No you're not. It's almost midnight and I haven't seen you for three *days!*

The night sky was blanketed by clouds; a shower was imminent, and it was already starting to sprinkle. Demons on the street hurried by, their heads covered by fans or top hats. Women kept the ends of their dresses raised so as not to drag them over puddles. A zeppelin soared overhead, blinking an advertisement for a clothing line and warning of severe weather. There was a homeless man huddled by a dumpster, covered by a tattered petticoat. I hailed a guard by the door, signaling for him to remove the unpleasant scenery. Lochai's poverty was bleeding into my layer. More and more people crossed the borders by illegal transit, and I feared that soon Tehlor would look like Avernai.

But that was a problem for another day. First, Persephone.

I'll be home soon, I promise. Our production is proving more challenging than I thought.

That bad?

Think of a nightmare within a nightmare. A layer *of nightmares.*

I'll wait two more hours, then I'm going to bed.

That's a bet. See you soon.

I watched the guard drag the crying homeless man out into the rain. I didn't like doing that, but a bleeding heart would only give me crowds of homeless camping under Garivel Theater by next week. I couldn't take care of every dredge down on his luck, not if they were coming in from other places. That was Lucifer's bit, and he was doing a piss-poor job of it.

I threw the cigarette down, mashing it with my boot. The door opened and my stagehand poked his head outside.

"Sir, are you ready? It's getting late and I only have one more go in me."

"Yeah, be there in a second."

He nodded and closed the door, and I gazed at the sky again. Multicolored lights from taprooms along the main street decorated the horizon with pale oranges, reds and greens, like the faintest rainbow on a stormy day. Laughter was carried with the wind, while music blared from audio posts and would continue to do so until early morning. Tehlor's nightlife was something to talk about. After all, I had a title to keep.

But I didn't feel as merry as I should, and there was something ominous in the air. I couldn't place my finger on it, as the feeling came and went far too quickly to catch. I leaned against my cane, reaching for the door. Throwing it open, I gave a slow exhale, ready to endure one more hour of pain.

***

In the early morning, Persephone lay in bed beside me, her naked, sleeping body wrapped in sheets. She always slept on her stomach with a leg curled beneath her. It looked horribly uncomfortable.

Her long, ruby-red hair was splayed in every direction, reaching across the bed to tickle my arm. I idly swept it away, my attention remaining on the cluster of sheets in my hand.

Persephone had come to Durn Manor ten years ago, applying for a maid position. She was the daughter of a poor watchmaker from Avernai, who turned her out the moment she was old enough to work. Her talents were limited, her ability to clean virtually non-existent, but I had hired her anyway. Eventually the only service she provided was to *me*, personally, in our bedroom.

Somewhere down the road, lust turned to love. I don't know when it happened, but having a partner wasn't as bad as I'd thought. When Persephone wasn't nagging me to come home, she was spontaneous and intelligent, and sometimes we talked all night about little things that no one else would ever care about.

I read over the Maiden and the Bear script for the umpteenth time, ignoring the weight of my eyelids. I should have been in bed hours ago, but desperation led to deprivation, and I was determined to save this production yet.

A knock at the door startled me awake. Exhaustion had won and I'd fallen asleep with the script in my hand. I grimaced, trying to determine whether the knock had been a dream. But then it happened again.

Three raps, in quick succession.

"Sir," said a whisper. It was Dreisel. "Sir, are you awake?"

"One second," I grumbled, throwing off the sheets and trudging to the door. Persephone stirred, but didn't wake.

I cracked open the door. Dreisel stood on the other side of it, his look relaying urgency. He, too, had been asleep, as his clothes were wrinkled and thrown on quickly. His hair was disheveled and his face was plagued with fatigue lines.

"I'm sorry to disturb you," he whispered, casting an easy glance at Persephone, as surely there'd be hell to pay if she was woken up. "But Samnaea Soran is in your foyer."

"… Samnaea Soran? Whatever for?"

"I don't know, sir, but she has guards. *Obsidian Court* guards."

That took a moment to process, and then I nodded. "Thank you, Dreisel. Keep them company until I get down there, yeah?"

"Of course, sir."

I shut the door and smoothed my air, making my way to the closet. Samnaea's visit should have come as a surprise, but it didn't. As crazy as that cow was, she wasn't stupid. Given enough time to stew, she'd put all the puzzle pieces together. Thankfully it was her word against mine, and the Jury would never let me hang.

I emerged from the hall and descended the stairs in a top hat and cream suit, cane at the ready. Samnaea waited at the bottom, a row of guards behind her, watching my entrance with a raised brow. A malay cigarette smoked from a thin silver holder between the fingers of her left hand, her ice blond hair shining unnaturally in the chandelier light. She wore a scarlet coat that reached her boots, a tulan-fur hood hugging her neck-line.

"Put that out," I said, frowning at the cigarette. "There's no smoking in here."

Samnaea dropped the cigarette on my floor, stamping it out with her foot. I glared at her. "Belial Vakkar, you are under arrest for high treason against the Court. I've afforded your arrest some privacy—given the hour—and you'd do well to come quietly so your subjects never discover what a disgusting snake you really are."

I laughed, leaning on the rail. "Oh, am I? And since when can one Archdemon arrest another? Why don't you come back with a general, and then we'll talk."

Samnaea reached into her pocket and lifted a tiny leather case. It flipped open, revealing the Obsidian crest. One glance, and all amusement drained from me like water through a sieve.

"... You're shitting me."

"Afraid not," she said, smiling. "Will you come quietly?"

I sneered, holding up my hands as a guard approached with cuffs. "Quietly, no. Care to explain what *high treason* entails?"

"Your crimes will be read aloud in Akkaroz. You can debate them there."

Dreisel watched my arrest, crestfallen.

"Belial?" came a voice from the top of the stairs. Persephone looked down at us, huddling into her violet sleep-robe. "What's happening?"

"Nothing, my dear," I muttered as the guards led me to the door. "Go back to bed; this will all be cleared up by morning."

"Wait!" Persephone cried, ignoring my advice. She hurried down the steps, but another group of guards stopped her approach, holding her at the bottom. "Why are you being arrested?" She looked up at a guard, frantic. "What has he done?"

"I've done nothing," I said, staring knives at *General* Soran. "I'm being framed for the stupidity of her brother is all."

Samnaea's smile turned frigid.

Without warning, Persephone's head exploded.

Startled, the guards dropped her body, trying to wipe away the gore on their armor. All they did was smear it around even more.

I stared down at Persephone's headless corpse, stung. The hollow feeling filled with shards of glass as despair and fury coalesced.

The guards holding me looked at each other, their expressions showing unease for what they'd witnessed. Lucifer had made a grave mistake by choosing her, but his biggest mistake lay in crossing *me*.

I broke the cuffs with just a tug, and the guards stepped back, alarmed. As they reached for their weapons I turned on them, snapping one of their necks, disarming the other, knocking him out with the handle of his own gun. I spun, sniping the remaining guards between the eyes. All of this had happened in a fraction of a minute.

Samnaea squinted, and I felt a tug on the back of my mind. But she wouldn't explode my head. She couldn't. And once she figured that out, her anger turned to fear and she backed for the door.

"What are you?" she snarled, but that demand was stunted by the quaver in her voice.

"Like you," I said, grinning. "Better than you, my dear. *Stronger* than you, *smarter* than you." Unlike the other select few, I hadn't gone public with my psionicity. A good thing, too, or else I might have been in some real trouble here. "But the act is just beginning, love. Let me show you what happens to cheeky cunts who barge in uninvited and destroy my property."

My sight flashed crimson, and there were starbursts behind my eyes. Samnaea witnessed that effect, as she gasped and reached for the door. Before she could escape, the walls erupted in a bed of flames, fire licking every inch of my home. The smell of burning upholstery mingled with searing flesh, and I watched delightedly as she dived through a window, screaming into the night.

Bitch.

But now I was a fugitive, and there was only one type of punishment dealt for violence against a Court superior.

As my life burned away, I stalked toward my study. The flames bent around me, my lungs immune to the searing, oxygen-deprived air. A steel-plated chest lay in the corner, shrouded in smoke, sealed by an electronic lock. I knelt, punching in the code with a squint.

I grabbed as much of its contents as my pockets could carry, tucking my most prized piece, a gold revolver, into my belt. Getting back on my feet was painful without my cane, and once there I paused, paying Persephone a final thought.

I'd loved her. *Pity.*

And then I headed for the back entrance port, destination *cephalon.* Purgatory was my only chance, and hopefully the Jury could wipe the penalty of execution off the slate.

The world would never see *The Maiden and the Bear.*

All for the better, probably.

V

EXHILED; QUEEN OF NOTHING

Leid Koseling—;

LOCHAI'S PRISON WAS DANK WITH ROT, PLAGUED by the scent of mildew and musk, the air like icy nails across my skin.

I'd made my way here straight from Caia, my clothes still damp with rain and blood. A guard led me to Namah Ipsin's quarters, the last cell amid a hall of many. Most of them were empty.

The guard opened the door and left, assured that I could fend for myself if Namah tried to flee. But I knew he wouldn't. He was here because he wanted to be here, and I intended to find out why.

Namah lay huddled on the bench, adorned in chains. A meal tray sat beside him, untouched. Shadows kept most of him concealed, but the yellow glow of his eyes burned on me the moment I entered. I could still remember him before the Ring War; before the Fall. The nihilistic angel doctor who was much kinder than he'd ever let on. Remembering those times always left me heartsick.

"I was expecting you sooner," he said, and despite the rest of him, his voice hadn't changed a bit.

I took a seat, silent.

"Did you find him?"

"How did you know?" I asked.

Namah leaned forward, emerging from the shadows. Greasy brown hair clung to his forehead, and his once handsome face was now withered by fatigue and years of stress. It pained me to see him so. Up until a week ago he had been the Archdemon of Lochai, but the code violation of Jerusalem, Earth had fated his execution. Namah would hang tomorrow.

"I've known for quite some time," he confessed, smiling weakly. "Spent years debating what to do."

"How?"

"Ixiah."

I recoiled. "He knew."

Namah nodded. "His noble lied to you. Qaira didn't die."

I looked away, wincing at the thought of all this time—so many years—Qaira had been locked up in that galactic prison, mind raped and made subservient to the Anakaari. It was a fate almost worse than death.

Damn you, Calenus.

"Is he here?" asked Namah.

"You sound hopeful."

"Is he?"

I thought of Alezair, lying unconscious in Cerasaraelia. Soon he would wake up to a new life. An *old* life, really, but that was something he could never know. And even though Qaira was here with me again, it still felt like he was dead. Because he *was* dead, and Alezair wore his corpse. It was both painful and beautiful to look at him, and whenever I did I was torn between laughter and sobs. Likewise, I hated and loved Namah for reuniting us.

Life was fickle.

"Why did you do it?" I asked, shelving his question.

"Something has to change," he murmured, looking to the barred window above us. "Everything is collapsing, layer by layer, and I believe that this is the first step…"

"The first step to what?"

He smiled. "I don't know; just a feeling. Don't you feel it?"

I did. Ever since I'd brought Alezair here, the air felt lighter. *Heady.* The feeling was ironic, given who he really was. "Namah,"

I sighed, "are you sure you want to go through with this? I can motion for a pardon—"

"No, I'm done," he snapped. "I've seen all I want to of this world. I don't belong here anymore. No one does, but they won't admit it."

He had never recovered from the Fall. The subsequent years of war and death were too much for him. I'd caught it from hearsay, but never understood the full extent of his burden until now. I wanted to beg him to reconsider, but knew that I had no right to impede on his decision. I had no right to force him to live. Instead I nodded, getting to my feet. Namah had given me all the answers I'd sought.

"Thank you," I said, fighting tears.

"My pleasure, Justice Commander," he replied, near whisper. "I only hope I've done the right thing."

***

The foul air turned sweet, and my eyes fluttered open.

Blood tears trickled down my face, their presence warm and thick. I wiped them away and stared at my bedroom ceiling, the darkness of Lochai's prison fading from view.

History was like tiny metal shards, piling atop one another, *elongating*, forming a sturdy blade. Time and tragedy had worn it dull, coated it in rust, yet that blade still managed to cut me every time.

And its cuts were always deep—straight to the heart. From it poured memories of what had been, even more painful were the hopeless reveries of what could have been. *Should have been.*

The heartache diminished as confusion settled in. I couldn't remember how I'd gotten here. And then I realized that my bedroom door was gone.

No, not gone; in pieces, scattered across the floor.

I shot up, and the sudden action left me lightheaded. I collapsed against the pillow, holding my head, fighting vertigo.

Every little movement caused tremors in my muscles. The ache was frightening.

I crawled from bed, slowly this time, my hands raking over splinters of wood as I made my way to the hall. Paintings and lamps were strewn everywhere, and the staircase railing was annihilated. I grabbed what was left and pulled myself to a stand, wincing as the ache intensified. My head pounded and my feet tingled, making it difficult to walk. I waited for the fatigue to pass, and it was then when I remembered the meeting with Yahweh and his generals, the sudden nosebleed and the darkness. I'd collapsed.

That meant they knew.

Oh god, they *knew*.

I slid down the stairs legs first, knowing if I tried it the normal way I'd break my neck. It wouldn't kill me, but a broken neck felt extremely unpleasant, Vel'Haru or not.

Our front door was broken, too. Blood was smeared across the frame, and I sank into a large depression in the wall. It was the shape of someone's body. What the hell had happened?

My ears caught sound of whispers from the kitchen. Frightened, panicked whispers. Amid their conversation, one word was repeated over and over again:

Alezair.

I scaled the dining room until I was leant against the kitchen doorframe. Adrial and Zhevraine were arguing. Neither of them saw me yet.

I listened, trying to get an idea of what had happened before they spotted me and spun the truth. Alezair wasn't here. He wasn't in Cerasaraelia at all; I couldn't feel him.

Before anything more was said, Zhevraine caught sight of me. Her mouth froze, eyes widened, and her expression cued Adrial to turn. He didn't seem as surprised.

"Welcome back," he said.

I pointed at the door with a trembling hand. "What happened to our house?"

The look my guardians shared was as if they were saying, *'You tell her. No, you.'*

"Where's Alezair?" I continued, not giving either of them a chance to explain.

Adrial sighed, nodding at the dining table. He plucked a bottle of wine from the liquor cabinet and Zhevraine brought three glasses. "Take a seat. We've got some things to discuss."

***

The rest of the afternoon was a haze. I spent most of it on my bedroom couch, staring at Qaira's violin case. For centuries, that violin had been my only keepsake, aside from the marriage vows that I continued to ink on my arms.

After all that had happened, and even in death, I'd never loved another man so much. And when Alezair appeared in Jerusalem, stalking me thereafter, I couldn't just discard him. I couldn't kill him like our code had ordered. *Not him,* that poor shell of a man, with no memories of the life he'd lost. I'd already done him in enough.

So I kept him, a small part of me always hoping that one day he'd remember. But he never did. He couldn't. The Nexus had scraped out his mind and programmed him human, and soon the mere sight of him hurt worse than anything.

God, *my heart.*

Tears brimmed my eyes and I winced, reaching for the pipe on the couch arm. But nothing numbed the ache. Soon Qaira would know himself, if not already, and then what? What would he do? Would he come back?

I hoped not. Just the thought of facing him was unbearable.

And in the midst of it all, my time was running out. Any day now I'd fall permanently unconscious, and my guardians would carry me back to Exo'daius for execution. *Euthanasia.* There were worse kinds of death, but I wasn't ready.

The Aeon chimed somewhere downstairs. I didn't move.

A moment later, Zhevraine appeared. "Yahweh Telei is on hold," she announced. When I didn't respond, she said, "It's urgent."

I forced myself off the couch and headed to the library, all the while debating to tell Yahweh the news. He deserved a warning.

After all I'd given a vengeful man the powers of near-invincibility. Should Qaira come looking for blood, Yahweh was defenseless. He and Lucifer both.

Neither of them had said a thing. I wasn't sure if they even knew what to say. Their level of silence was shocking, as I'd anticipated uproar at the sight of Alezair sitting behind that podium. I'd tried to hide him by prolonging his training, but I couldn't keep him caged in Purgatory forever. And the more I thought about it, the more I knew how inevitable this all had been.

I touched the rune on the Aeon, exhaling slowly.

Hello, Yahweh.

I'm sorry to call your home, outside business hours no less. I tried the Celestial Court first.

Don't apologize. What's the matter?

We need to meet. Tonight. Something's happened and I can't really talk right now. The Argent Court is up in arms and I'm expected at the Grand Hall for a statement in ten minutes.

A statement for what?

... The Contest is over, Leid. Lucifer withdrew Hell's participation this afternoon. He's declared war on Heaven.

I said nothing, staring at the wall. Seams were unraveling all at once.

Can we meet? he pressed.

Yes, um, why don't you and your generals have dinner with us? We sit down in two hours, or is that too soon?

Two hours is manageable. I'll see you then.

As I removed my finger from Crylle's rune, Adrial burst into the library. He looked distraught. "Commander Raith is making a speech over Hell's airwaves. He's declaring war on Heaven. It's on *every* channel."

I hung my head, closed my eyes. "Yes, I know. Yahweh just informed me."

When I said nothing else, he held out his hands. "What are we going to do?"

"I don't know yet. Yahweh and his generals will be here in a couple of hours and we can get the full story then."

But that wasn't what Adrial meant. Our contract ended with the Contest. If Lucifer repealed the Contest, then our asylum here was null. Our options were to scour the Multiverse in search of a new home—a new life—or return to Exo'daius, tails tucked between our legs.

No.

I couldn't think about this now. Too many other things were happening.

Adrial continued to speak, but I didn't hear him. His words were nothing but white noise amid a tangle of barely-coherent thoughts.

I pushed by him with a raised hand, a gesture for silence. I needed quiet, solitude.

The garden.

***

Moritoria had changed over the years; the temples and Acolytes of Maghir lost to time and irreverence, buried with Sanctum and its people.

Left behind was the city of Adure, isolated yet intact, the garden offering a clear view of the ornate pillars and domiciles from Cerasaraelia's escarpment. Alezair had worn a look when I toured him through there. He'd seen it many times before; we were married only half a mile away.

But what hadn't changed was the gray sky and ever-present blanket of fog. Although such monotony was usually maddening, today I found the scenery ataractic. It offered a glimmer of hope, on some level.

Seated on a marble bench with a cigarette smoking between my fingers, I thought of how to mend Heaven and Hell's alliance.

Lucifer had already made a statement, and he was a rational man—much more so than his peers. That meant he'd given war a lot of thought, and the chances of convincing him to renege were slim to none. I could get Telei and Raith to sit down, negotiate, but the fact that they were unable to do that of their own accord was…strange. *Troubling.*

I winced as the cigarette singed my fingers. It had burned all the way to the filter, and I released it. It fell to the cement with a tiny bounce, extinguishing soon after.

I was so tired; all I wanted to do was crawl back into bed and pretend that none of this ever happened. My lids felt heavy and I appeased them, closing my eyes for only a minute. My body hummed with exhaustion as the world fell away, and I floated in between consciousness, like a lucid dream.

When I opened my eyes, someone was standing in front of me.

Belial Vakkar, covered in blood and soot. At my confusion, he swallowed hard and removed his top hat, wiping away the black smudges on his face. His usual, vainglorious air was gone. Now he was gloomy, subdued.

"We have a problem, Justice," he said. "A *big* problem."

TITLES IN THE HYMN OF THE MULTIVERSE:

This series is on-going. Can't wait for the next *Hymn of the Multiverse* installment? Sign up to receive an email notification whenever a new book drops: http://eepurl.com/dDFIy5

(THE ANTITHESIS)
1 – INCEPTION
2 – HONOR
3 – FALLEN
4 – WAR
5 – VENGEANCE
(DYSPHORIA)
1 – RISE
2 – PERMANENCE (4/2019)

You can also connect through facebook:
https://www.facebook.com/terrawhitemanscifi/